It Can't
Happen to Me

It Can't Happen to Me

C. Ellen Watts

STANDARD PUBLISHING

Cincinnati, Ohio

24-03996

Standard Contemporary Fiction Series
for Teens

Runaway! / *Janet Willig*
Moving Again! I'm Not Going / *C. Ellen Watts*
Wise Up, Zack / *Michael P. Murphy*
Songs in the Night / *Carol Farley*
You're So Immature / *Robert E. Korth*
It Can't Happen to Me / *C. Ellen Watts*

Library of Congress Cataloging-in-Publication Data

Watts, C. Ellen.
    It can't happen to me / C. Ellen Watts
      p. cm.
    Summary: After accepting a ride from a stranger who tried to abduct and sexually molest her, fourteen-year-old Pippa deals with her feelings of guilt, self-recrimination, and fear.
    ISBN 0-87403-756-5
    [1. Strangers--Fiction. 2. Child molesting--Fiction. 3. Christian life--Fiction.] I. Title.
    PZ7.W334It   1990
    [Fic--dc20]   90-34017
                                          CIP
                                          AC

to
The Fearless Four—
Kara, Sara, Stacie, and Michael

1

It was Martin Luther King's birthday and a school holiday and I didn't have to babysit. Mom's a teacher and all the schools were out for the day. She would watch Jaime for a change while I went to the mall with Maryjo and Robyn. We planned to meet at the fountain and eat lunch together. Then we would goof around and shop all afternoon without my little sister tagging along.

"Be home by five," Mom called as I hollered, "I'm leaving now," and hurried out the front door.

Fairview Mall was in the newer section of town, a few blocks from where we lived on Pepperidge Lane. Although the temperature wasn't bad for January, the wind was nippy. I zipped my ski jacket up to my chin and wrapped my old plaid scarf around my neck.

I was steaming along, wishing I'd thought to wear my furry earmuffs, when I heard the quick beep of a horn. A white van pulled over to the curb and stopped beside a NO PARKING sign. The passenger door opened and a man leaned across the seat and motioned to me.

"Pippa—P.J.?" he said, using my nickname, "Your dad needs you at the office."

Dad was a certified public accountant (CPA). January was when what seemed like the whole city began clamoring all at once to have their income tax figured. Except for Sundays and the nights he bowled, Dad hardly took time off to breathe until after mid-April. Sometimes I helped out by running the copy machine after school.

I frowned. The evening before, over two scoops of Cherry Delight topped with nuts and whipped cream (Dad's one brief holiday celebration with the rest of us), I had asked Dad if he needed me to work or could I make other plans. After teasing me a bit, he'd said to go ahead and have a fun day. The least he could have done, if he'd changed his mind, was to phone and say so before I'd walked halfway to the mall in a sleet storm. And how come he'd sent some gray-haired old gink I didn't even know?

"Are you sure?" I asked crossly. I hardly ever got to go to the mall with my friends.

"Am I sure? Listen to her. There's enough copy work piled on Daddy's desk to keep you humping all day. Come on, get in," the man in the van coaxed.

"How do I know you work with my dad? I don't even know you," I said. I was being rude, I knew, but I couldn't help it.

"Apologies. I'm Floyd. Floyd Conner," he said. I guess I figured everyone knew old Floyd."

"Well, I don't," I started to say. However, if he was Dad's co-worker, I could at least be polite. Burrowing my cold hands deep inside my pockets, I said without enthusiasm, "It's nice to meet you."

"And I say it's lucky meeting you. Your daddy said, 'Go to the house,' so I drove there first. Your mamma said to hurry and I might catch up with you on Fairview. It's a good thing I did. I'd've had me a time trying to find you in that mall. But here I am talking and you're freezing." He patted the bucket seat. "Get in P.K.—uh, P.J. We'll have you helping Daddy in no time."

His voice had an unpleasant nasal twang. Although the wind had started to blow harder, something held me back. I had been in Dad's office once or twice a week for the last two years and I thought I knew the twenty or so people who worked there. I sure didn't know anyone by the name of Floyd Conner. But if Dad needed me to work, I'd work.

The gusty wind whipped around the van, bringing tears to my eyes. Holding my scarf up over my mouth, I mumbled through woolen layers, "I can walk. Thanks anyhow."

The stranger's bushy eyebrows shot up. "In this weather? Look at your hands. They're red as fire trucks."

I'd lost my good mittens and my old ones had holes in the thumbs. Now I wished I'd worn the old ones anyhow. Floyd Conner was right—it was too cold to be walking.

Keeping my feet planted firmly on the icy sidewalk, hunching against the wind, I hugged my arms to my sides, swiveled, and peered down Fairview. It had to be a mile or more to Dad's downtown office.

Tiny prickles of sleet danced across the van's hood and stung my face and forehead.

Floyd Conner told me, "Will Howard—your daddy—says you're the best office help he's ever had, by george. He was saying to me just yesterday how he's thinking of upping your pay."

Dad paid me minimum wage, which was more than I got for babysitting Jaime. A raise would be great.

A horn sounded behind the van, then another. I glanced at the NO PARKING sign.

The man asked, "Are you coming or aren't you?"

A taxi nose-dived to a stop behind the other two cars, then darted to fill a traffic gap in the inside lane. The man stopped behind us cranked down his window and swore. I couldn't just stand there like a dummy. Besides, I'd been taught to obey my elders and to respect old age.

The van was the older type. I had to step really high to get in. I slammed the door shut and, cold or no cold, immediately wished myself back on the sidewalk.

As I reached for the seat belt, Floyd grabbed ahold of the floor shift, pulled rapidly away from the curb, and entered the flow of traffic. As he swung around a slow-moving bread truck, I grasped the seat with both hands and clung.

Floyd let go of the gearshift and patted my hand. "Smart kid—just like Daddy said."

I didn't like being touched by people I didn't know. As his hand started to close around mine, I let go of the seat and reached up and loosened my scarf. Then, for the first time, I turned and really looked at Floyd Conner. He wasn't as old as I'd thought. But it had been hard to see with sleet coming at me like crazy.

The hood of his gray corduroy work-type coat was unzipped, revealing a thatch of longish gray hair. Although neatly parted near the middle and combed back on either side in front, the back looked as if it could stand a double shampoo. His plump face seemed vaguely familiar, though I couldn't recall having seen him before. The deep brown lines on either side of his mouth looked as if they'd been penciled in with eye makeup. Probably he chewed tobacco. Yuk.

He pawed once more for my hand.

Cool it, Pop! I may look like a cute little kid, but I'm fourteen years old. I'm practically—

"You like what you see?" he asked.

His tone frightened me. At the same time, I was embarrassed. I hadn't meant to stare. Only at Dad's office they had a dress code and everything. Floyd had on a plaid shirt with no tie and he was wearing khaki trousers. Neat enough, but hardly within the code. Probably he was a custodian, or maybe it was his day off.

That was highly unlikely. *Nobody* got extra days off during income tax time.

He couldn't be a janitor either. I'd been there in the fall the day Dad hired a cleaning service run by housewives.

As we approached the mall, my stomach churned. I knew I should mind my dad. Like it or not, that probably included riding downtown with Floyd Conner. It was also unfair to judge a person by his outward appearance. Still—

The sleet had turned to icy needles mixed with rain. Floyd started the wipers.

"I was supposed to meet my friends here," I said. "Can we stop long enough for me to go by the fountain and tell them I have to work?"

He might be the grandpa type, he might even be Dad's best friend. I couldn't help it, I was scared of Floyd Conner. Once I was out of the van, nothing or no one could entice me to get back in.

"No!"

Startled by his sudden vehemence, I shrank against the door. Pushing a finger tight against my upper lip, I begged, "Please, let me out. You won't have to wait. I can walk. I've done it before."

"You think I'm crazy?" he shouted. "No, we're not stopping."

As quickly as it had arisen, his anger cooled. "I didn't mean to scare you, Honey," he soothed. "But your daddy said to hurry; he's in a real bind."

We passed the mall and stopped at a traffic light. The stranger turned toward me and slowly licked his lips. He had a funny look in his greenish eyes. Not ha-ha funny. Weird.

"Pippa, you look like a scared little bird squeezed over next to the door like that. A pretty bird, of course—real pretty. Don't be scared. Nothin's gonna hurt you."

The light changed. He shifted more smoothly as he talked on. "I caught me a little bird once—brown and shiny as your hair. A young one. It had black eyes—like little beads they were. Yours are blue, ain't they? And feathers soft as a baby's blanket. All the time I was holding that little bird. I could feel its little heart going pitty-pat, pitty-pat . . ."

His voice dropped to a singsong. He kept looking over at me until my heart hammered so hard I was sure he could hear it. Clamping my feet against the floor boards and my knees together, I forced my hands to lie quietly in my lap.

Stupid! Stupid! Stupid! The words inside my head were like the clang of a fire alarm.

"You're a pretty girl, P.J." he repeated. "I like pretty girls." The van skidded sideways.

Please, God, hurry, get us there! "Watch where you're going!" I scolded. "It's getting slick."

He chuckled and patted my knee. "Spunky, too. Nothin' like a spunky woman."

As I jerked away, I kicked against something on the floor. Glancing down, thinking to move whatever it was so I could keep out of Floyd's reach, I shivered. A one-eyed snake with triple tongues stared sightlessly at me from the brass-tipped toe of a neatly polished cowboy boot. Brilliant red stones glittered from the eye's center. The reptile's scaly long tail was wrapped around what appeared to be a green-eyed mermaid. A second boot lay against the console. I closed my eyes and shuddered.

"Cold, Sweetheart?"

Cold? What was cold when I was the scaredest I had ever been in my life? "No, I'm fine," I lied.

Ahead I could see Taco Bell and Miller's Drugstore where you turned and went half a block to Dad's office. The traffic light was red. Floyd pulled into the left turn lane and stopped. Relief washed over me like summer sun. In a moment we'd be there and I could get out of the van and walk away from slimy, awful Floyd Conner forever.

The light turned amber, then green. Floyd stomped on the gas and the van shot away from the turn lane and across the intersection ahead of the rest of the traffic.

"Mr. Conner, you were supposed to turn there. You missed the turn," I yelled.

He slowed down a little. "I'm taking the shortcut," he said.

"No you're not!" Anyone who knew anything at all about downtown knew you couldn't turn left for at least six blocks. We were not going to Dad's office.

Fear turned to sickening terror as Floyd leered at me, licked his lips, and said, "Maybe we'll just go for a little ride. You'd like that, wouldn't you? You'll like riding with big Floyd."

"Please," I whimpered. "I want to go help Daddy."

Floyd Conner kept right on driving.

2

It seemed as if I had been trapped inside the old white van forever. In reality, it could not have been for more than ten minutes. I counted the blocks from Taco Bell to where Floyd made a right turn off Fairview. Seven in all.

Through the lighted windows of the houses in the mostly residential area, I saw kids in front of TVs or gathered around tables eating lunch. In one house a boy stood near a table with his back to the window. From his movements, and the shape of the jar in front of him, I guessed he was making himself a peanut butter sandwich. I wished I was home doing the same.

If only a police car would come!

But it was not one of those holidays when our whole police force turns out because of drunken drivers. Kids were

14

out of school and the post office was closed. Except for banks and such, that was about it. The nasty weather had made it so even folks who might otherwise have been out shopping had chosen instead to stay indoors.

Twice a year, September and March, kindergarten through grade school, a soft-spoken police officer had visited our school and talked to us about getting to and from school safely. I had heard "Never get into a car with a stranger" as often as I had sung "The Star-Spangled Banner." Now I was in eighth grade and what had I done? Exactly what I'd been told never to do.

As the sleet beat against the windows, my thoughts became a mixture of fear and gloom. I had read abduction stories in the papers and heard them on TV news. What if that happened to me?

The door handle was like the cold steel barrel of a gun against my ribs. Stifling a whimper, I shifted positions and prayed we'd meet a police car. We didn't.

Tucked among some school pictures in my wallet was a tattered newspaper clipping listing Oren Richardson's name along with the rest of MacArthur Junior High's A team. It was the only paper I had. Even if it had a margin to write on, I'd have died before giving up that particular two-inch square of newsprint. Besides, even if I dropped a note out the window, who was there to find it? The streets were deserted.

Staring straight ahead, yet speaking to Floyd Conner, I said, "If I don't show up at the mall, my friends will call Mom. She'll phone Dad and they'll start looking for me."

Actually, if Dad thought anything had happened to either Jaime or me, he probably wouldn't have hesitated to call in the FBI.

Floyd's voice was as smooth as Jello pudding. "They won't know where to look."

"My mom—" I stopped. Inner instinct told me Mom had

never even seen that van. Neither had she seen Floyd. He had lied about going to the house. And I was almost positive he had lied to me about Dad, too. Only if that were so, how come Floyd knew my name and that I did copy work for Dad?

I hate the way you lick your lips, I wanted to scream at him.

"They *never* know where to look," he said softly.

Sick with dread over what he had hinted at, I wondered. If mine was not his first abduction, who were the others? Where were they? What had happened to them?

With my heart in my throat, I lashed angrily out at him. "You've got no right to take me where I don't want to go. I don't even know you!"

Floyd responded with an eerie chuckle. He kept cackling in the same strange, high voice for almost a whole block. Then he touched the turn signal.

The street sign loomed before me. *Oh, Lord, please— not Lombardy!*

I knew the street well. Out near the end, after the houses had thinned and then dwindled to none, there was a small stadium and ball field used mostly by the Little League. Across from the stadium was the entrance to Riverside golf course. Beyond it was the familiar winding strip of land known as Riverside Park. Left pretty much in its natural state, what had been the town's first park was covered with gigantic trees and overgrown shrubs.

As we neared the ball field, I scanned both sides of the street for signs of life. The entire area was deserted, as it always was in the dead of winter. Who in their right mind would be at the park on a day like this?

We jounced across the grating beneath the ironwork archway that marked the park's entrance. As we passed by clumps of ice-laden evergreen, a cottontail rabbit jumped and ran across the narrow blacktop road in front of us. Floyd swore and veered sharply to the right, narrowly missing a huge balsam.

You creep. You'd wreck the dumb van before you'd hit an animal, I whimpered silently. *But you don't care what happens to me.*

For a moment Floyd continued to curse the rabbit. Then his mood changed and he let up a little on the accelerator. He stopped swearing and began saying foul, suggestive things to me.

My stomach heaved. I hated the swear words, but anything was better than the vile language he was using now.

I put my hands over my ears. "Stop it," I blubbered. "I don't have to listen to that kind of garbage."

Floyd acted as if he were in a trance, like he hadn't even heard me. Still spewing those awful words, he groped across the console, touching me where I had no wish to be touched.

"Stop it! Don't!" I screamed, squirming to move beyond his reach.

As frightened as I was, something said I should sit still, so I could think more clearly. With all that gray hair, Floyd Conner had to be considerably older than my dad, and I was a good runner. The next time Floyd glanced at the road, I quietly unbuckled my seat belt.

As we approached the next curve, I jammed down hard on the handle, swung the door wide, and jumped.

My plan was to come up running and disappear into the brush. I did manage to land on my feet, but the roadside was icy and my feet slipped out from under me. I hit the ground and rolled over and over, coming to rest laying face down on the gravel near the roots of a giant oak. For an instant everything went black.

As if from a distance. I heard the screeching of brakes followed by the sound of rapid shifting and the whine of the van's engine. I looked up to see it backing rapidly toward me.

Icy gravel bit into my palms as I scrambled to right myself. Before I could get up, the right rear wheel bounced over my left arm. There was a sickening crunch and a stab of pain shot to the tips of my fingers, through my shoulder, and clear to the top of my head.

My mouth and nose hit the gravel and I could taste blood as I struggled to keep from losing consciousness again.

I heard the van door creak open and heavy footsteps crunching against the icy blacktop. Floyd stopped somewhere behind me. I held my breath. A rasping of heavy hinges announced the opening of the back doors.

Still flat on my face and fighting panic, I kept my eyes closed, faking unconsciousness. My stomach heaved.

His voice was harsh and hurried. "C'mon, kid. Get up."

When I didn't, he prodded me with a heavy work shoe. "I said to get up!"

Why, why had I waited for a remote place like Riverside Park to decide to jump out?

Gritting my teeth against the pain, I pushed up with my good arm and struggled to my feet. Before I could take even a single step, Floyd's arms tightened around me from behind.

Twisting sideways, I punched him as hard as I could with my good elbow. He grunted. During the struggle that followed, my left arm flopped until I thought I would faint.

"Can't you see my arm's broken," I panted. By then I was half-crazy with pain and so angry I could spit.

He paused and gasped for breath. "I never meant for you to get hurt."

I thought for a moment he might let me go. Then his arms tightened and he half-carried, half-dragged me to the back of the van.

Floyd's was not a passenger van but the kind used for hauling. It had no windows in back.

I had been afraid to scream. Now as he pushed and

shoved and hoisted me into the van, I let go with everything I had.

"Help! Somebody help!" Then, "Let me go! Help!"

I know for positive God heard me. Why else would I hear voices just as Floyd climbed into the van and clamped a rough hand over my bleeding mouth? Kids' voices.

Floyd heard them, too. Mouth open, panting like a hunted animal. He raised his head and listened.

Caught off guard, his hold on me loosened. I jerked sideways and sat up. We both saw them at the same time. Two boys on bicycles, slipping and sliding, laughing, and spinning their wheels on purpose on the slick roadway.

Floyd let go of me and made a dive for the front of the van. He had left the keys dangling from the ignition, the van running.

"Get down!" he hollered in a loud voice.

Instead, I sat the rest of the way up and scooted as fast as I could across the ragged carpet covering the van's floor. My feet touched the road just as the van roared away and I sat down hard.

3

The boys slid to a stop and stared. Dropping their bikes in the middle of the road, they ran to me.

"That man was making me go where I didn't want to go," I blubbered. They were just kids. I couldn't say what else I knew was probably about to happen. "Get help! Call the police. Hurry—before he comes back!"

The boys looked at each other. "You go. I'll stay with her," the larger boy said.

He fished in his pocket. "Here, Mike. Here's a quarter. There's a phone booth beside the gate at the fair grounds. Dial 911, that's fastest."

Mike's freckles nearly popped off his white face. "Did you get the license number?"

"There wasn't any plate," the older boy said. "Go on, get

going. But be careful, it's slick." he called as Mike took off in the direction of the park's entrance.

Squatting on the ground in front of me, he said, "Your arm's broken, isn't it? Even with your coat I can tell by the way it looks."

"I can tell by the way it feels," I snapped. I apologized. My crankiness was no more the boy's fault than anything else that had taken place. Cradling the injured arm with my other hand, I moved it slowly to where I could support it with my stomach and hunched up knees.

The roaring and rattling of the speeding van soon vanished, and the swishings of the bicycle were quickly swallowed by distance. A shower of ice fell from an over-laden branch, cascading onto the roadway. Then silence.

Agitated over the stupidity that had gotten me in such a mess, I was also embarrassed. What if the boys should ask questions? While they both seemed like nice kids, I didn't know either one of them. The boy on the ground alternated between staring at my skinned face and looking down the road for his friend.

"What's your name?" I asked.

"Brad Taylor."

"I'm Pippa Howard. P.J."

"Was that guy trying to rape you?" Brad asked right out of the blue.

I just about died. Brad could not have been more than eleven or twelve. How come he knew about stuff like that when I barely knew about it myself?

"No!" I lied.

While part of my brain scurried to scrape up an explanation that would satisfy him, I changed the subject. "How old are you, Brad?"

He gave me a funny look. I got the feeling he not only knew I had lied but that he was more grown up at the moment than I was.

"Eleven," he said quietly. "My friend's ten."

"I wish you'd seen his license number. If you could have memorized it, written it down—"

"Didn't you hear me? I couldn't see the front but I'm positive there was no plate on the back. How'd you break your arm and get your face so messed up?" he asked abruptly.

"Being stupid. I got out while the van was still moving. Don't ever do a crazy thing like that," I warned, not looking at him.

He waited until I risked a glance. Then his eyes caught mine and held. "How come you jumped?" he asked. "How come you were screaming?"

"How come you have to ask so many questions?" Part of my impatience was for real, the rest deliberate. "Like I said—he wanted me to go someplace I didn't want to go. I said to let me out. When he didn't stop fast enough to suit me, I jumped out. I knew better than to jump from a moving vehicle. It was a dumb thing to do." If I repeated it often enough, maybe I would believe it myself. Maybe I could stop wishing I'd had sense enough to jump out while we were still on Fairview. Or at the stoplight. Or even in town.

"Then how come he had you in the back of the van? How come he drove off so fast when he saw Mike and me? If he wasn't aiming to hurt you, how come he didn't stay and help you?"

"I don't know! Will you please stop asking me stuff I don't know?"

My feet were cold, and my shoulders. I started to shiver. Forcing myself to calm down. I said through chattering teeth, "I wish they'd hurry."

Brad got up and stretched and squatted down beside me. "Maybe I can help keep you warm. You're probably colder than I am. You're the one who's hurt," he said.

I had never been hysterical, but something told me I was

on the verge. Moaning softly, fighting to maintain self-control, I shut my eyes and nursed my arm. When at last we heard the wail of approaching sirens I opened my eyes and saw Mike pedaling carefully toward us. By then I could no longer control the shaking. My bottom felt frozen to the blacktop. Tears ran down my cheeks as I began to cry great gulping sobs that tore at my chest and aching arm and body.

The police arrived first, followed by the rescue unit. A fire truck lumbered a little ways behind. Still further back in the noisy, honking procession, I could see yet another police car. They probably wouldn't have turned on any more sirens if the Regency Hotel had been on fire.

A police officer got out of his car and came toward me. I tried hard to answer his rapid questions, but my head started to feel really strange and my words seemed oddly disconnected.

I repeated, "A man said I was supposed to go work for my dad so I got in but he didn't stop at Dad's office. He was taking me—I don't know where—I didn't want to go—and then—"

"I think he was trying to rape her," Brad said.

My back stiffened. "No, sir!"

I slumped against Brad, shivering. I began to whimper. The officer's voice faded in and out. Then I felt myself being lifted, and someone put a warm blanket over me and tucked it around me and strapped me onto a stretcher. Brad continued to talk to the officer. His voice, too, had grown so fuzzy I could no longer hear what he was saying.

They lifted the stretcher and pushed it between a pair of yawning white doors. I struggled against the straps.

"Don't. Please don't make me get back in the van," I begged.

It wasn't the van, of course. It was the rescue unit. But I didn't know that until later. All I knew was that I had once again been forced inside a strange vehicle. This time when the doors clicked shut, I didn't wait. I screamed and screamed. At least I think I did. But maybe it was just inside my head.

4

The woman's soothing voice repeated over and over again, "It's OK, Honey. You're safe now. Everything's going to be all right."

As her voice grew louder, the screaming stopped. After a little while I opened my eyes. The voice belonged to a young woman in a navy blue jumpsuit.

Cautiously moving my head, I scanned my surroundings. I said, "It's not the van."

"No, Honey. The van's gone. This is the rescue unit. We're on our way to the hospital."

"Can't you just take me home?"

"I'm sorry."

I didn't want to go to the hospital. I wanted to go home and go to my room and shut the door and be by myself and not have to answer questions or talk to anybody—maybe not ever. It was as if I had been smeared on by an extremely filthy person. The filth was of a sort that could not be washed off. It soaked through my skin and ran all through my insides where it clung and stank like rotten garbage.

While plenty went on that shouldn't have among some of the students at MacArthur Junior High where I went to school, I had never been a part of that crowd. Other than a few times when I hadn't known what was coming, I'd never even listened to anybody's dirty stories. And I didn't use bad words.

True, I had gotten into trouble at school a couple of times. That (according to Mr. Cordell, our principal) was because I had "allowed my exuberance to get ahead of my common sense." While I was no angel in a lot of other ways, I could think of nothing I had done to attract a weirdo like Floyd Conner. Still, I must have done something wrong. Otherwise, why would he choose me over thousands of other available girls?

By the time we'd reached the hospital I was what Mom would call a "basket case." Then, in the emergency room, they said I had to get undressed so they could examine me. Because of my arm, I couldn't undress myself. I had to be rolled around and turned like a two-year-old while a woman in a white outfit did it for me.

I didn't want to be examined, or even looked at, for that matter. They made me wear a crackly white paper gown that opened down the back like a cobbler apron. Even after I was back on the gurney, and all but my head was covered with a big paper sheet, I still felt naked. Probably every single one of the people who bustled in and out of the room knew I wasn't wearing a stitch. I will give them credit for one thing. They were all really gentle with my arm.

I had barely gotten settled under the sheet before the police officer came striding into emergency as if he had a perfect right. He sounded a little impatient with me when I said I couldn't remember what Floyd Conner looked like.

I was telling the truth, I couldn't remember. Although all that had happened was as real as the gurney beneath me, it was as if a black shade had been drawn inside my head. On one side of it I could see the string of events as they had happened that morning in brilliant technicolor and give all the right answers. The rest was a blank.

Relieved to discover I hadn't forgotten my name or our phone number or Dad's number at work, I also replied correctly that Dr. Thorpe had been our doctor since before I'd been born.

Dad's office was just a few blocks from the hospital and he didn't have Jaime to arrange for, so he got there before Mom did. They were still cleaning bits of gravel from my face when Dad came in. What's left of his hair was all wind-blown, and he had on what Mom called his "worry face." The minute I saw him, I started bawling again.

"If you needed me, why didn't you say so instead of sending that creepy Floyd Conner after me?" I stormed.

Dad's voice had a choky sound. "I didn't send anyone after you, Sweetheart. I don't even know a Floyd Conner— not that I can think of, anyhow. I thought I told you last night I wouldn't be needing your help today."

It was all so confusing, I didn't know whether to believe him or not. When Mom came in a few minutes later, part of me was glad to see her while the rest accused, "You told him where I was! How could you? You knew I didn't know him."

Mom, too, insisted she had never even seen a white van. And she would never have, not in hers or my wildest imaginings, ever have sent a stranger to get me. Surely I knew that.

After Dr. Thorpe arrived, the policeman ushered Mom and Dad into the hall and I could no longer hear what they were saying.

Dr. Thorpe moved like he'd been put together with brass fasteners, and he looked like a 20th-century Abe Lincoln—homely, but also very kind.

He looked soberly down at me for a moment. Then he brushed a bit of stray hair from off my scratched forehead. I couldn't say for sure, but I think I saw tears in his eyes. I guess I was special to him. He always said all the kids he'd delivered as babies were special.

"It's all right, P.J. You're going to be all right. Give me a minute to scrub and we'll have a look at that arm."

I heard water gurgling and smelled the strong odor of antiseptic followed by the rasping of paper towels being pulled from a dispenser.

"Sometimes you can get run over by a car and come off with hardly a bruise. You missed that kind of luck." he said.

There were X-rays to take and examine, and what seemed like endless poking and prodding and lifting and moving. At last he said, "You can be glad this is your left arm. It's going to need quite a cast. At least your art work won't be hindered."

One reason I liked Dr. Thorpe so much was because he treated me like a real person and not just a kid. He had hundreds of patients, several of them near my age. He still never forgot my name or what school I went to or my interest in becoming an artist.

"Some missionaries were at our church last month," I told him. "The lady slipped on some ice and broke her elbow in three places. They cut some slits and put it together with pins or something. She didn't have to have a cast. The bones healed really fast. Can't you do mine that way?"

Dr. Thorpe smiled. "A marvelous procedure," he said. "New and marvelous. But it won't work for you, I'm afraid. As nearly as I can tell, you have a total of four breaks and only one of them clean. Sorry. Now let's talk about what else is wrong with you."

"Just my face. It stings and it's starting to get stiff. They already fixed it," I said, and might have giggled at what that implied had he not looked so grave.

He spoke softly. "Pippa, the report is you were abducted. You've grown into a lovely young lady. You are no longer a child. I'm sure you are quite aware of what can happen during an abduction. If things took place that shouldn't have—if you were violated in any way—I need to know about it. So tell me, what happened?"

"Nothing." I could tell he didn't believe me.

"The boys who found you—they used a rather unpleasant word to describe what they thought had happened."

"Well, they were wrong!" I insisted.

"What did take place?"

"This weird guy picked me up in a van and took me where I didn't want to go. I jumped out. He ran over my arm. That's all."

I had started to sound like a parrot, I knew, but it couldn't be helped.

The doctor persisted. "Did he touch you?"

If I said yes, everyone in the world would soon know how stupid I'd been. If I said no, I would be lying. I chose the latter. The trouble was, I had always been so truthful, I didn't know how to tell a decent lie even when I needed to.

Fixing my eyes on the stethoscope dangling from Dr. Thorpe's neck, I mumbled, "Why would he want to touch me?"

"You tell me."

"I don't have anything to tell you."

Dr. Thorpe turned and swished away, and I could hear him murmuring along with my parents and the officer in the hall. I couldn't understand a word until Mom's voice rose hysterically.

"Doctor! I don't care what she said. We have to know. Please, examine her thoroughly."

With my good hand, I wadded the paper sheet under me. I began to cry. If even Mom was going to allow me to continue being humiliated, who was left to tuck in the sheet on the other side?

5

At Dr. Thorpe's insistence, I spent the night in the hospital. My folks agreed. I cried and carried on and begged them all to please, please let me go home. I might as well have saved all that energy. When Mom and Dad made up their minds on what they thought was best for me, it was as if I no longer had an opinion. Add Dr. Thorpe and the three were as immovable as the new and still-wet cast encasing my arm from my left thumb to my armpit and shoulder.

"You haven't had lunch," Mom realized, after two young men in what looked like white sweats had moved me to a regular room.

"Can't I be alone?" I asked, eyeing the empty bed beside mine.

"Ignore that one," Dad said. "Dr. Thorpe specifically ordered private. I heard him."

Mom continued to fuss about food. "The noon meal's been served," she said.

"Mom, I'm not hungry."

As if both my ears had been broken instead of my arm, she said to Dad, "The child has to eat, Will. Go get her something from the cafeteria."

"Don't. I won't eat it," I argued.

Dad returned after a little while carrying a fat chicken sandwich and a milkshake. I nibbled at the shredded lettuce sprangling from between thick slices of brown bread and gagged. I put it back in its styrofoam box and leaned back against the pillow.

"We'll try again later."

"She's had a bad experience. It's hard to eat when you've had a bad experience."

"Her arm probably hurts. Does it hurt much, P.J.?"

"No, and I wish you two would stop talking about me as if I'd gone to Australia. I can still hear, you know." I said crossly.

Around four o'clock Dad went home to relieve Davida who lived next door and was looking after Jaime. Davida was an only child. Her parents gave her $200 a month and let her buy her own clothes and everything. They were both psychiatrists and made a lot of money.

"How come Davida of all people? Davida never babysits."

"Because both Robyn and Maryjo were at the mall waiting for you," Mom reminded. "I had to have someone in a hurry. Davida was handy."

"I'll bet Jaime hates having her," I remarked.

"Why don't you see if you can rest, maybe take a little nap," Mom suggested.

"I'm not sleepy."

"Then perhaps you'd like to talk."

"About what?"

"You know—what happened."

I wished I'd either gone to sleep or faked it.

"You needn't, of course. But since Dad's gone and it's just us girls—"

"I don't feel like talking. Besides, I don't even know what *it* is that everyone all of a sudden wants me to talk about!"

She let me alone for a while. I switched on the TV and dozed through an old rerun of "Little House" while Mom leafed through a magazine she'd found out in the waiting room.

A pretty Filipino girl wearing a rose-colored uniform brought me dinner. I still choked at the sight of all that food. Mom said I should try to manage a few bites anyhow. I tried, but I still couldn't eat.

When Dad returned at seven, I said, "I'm glad you didn't bring Jaime."

"Why is that?" he asked.

Because even Jaime would know better than to get into a strange vehicle with someone she didn't know.

Aloud, I said, "I dunno. I'm just glad." Then, "Did you see Maryjo—or Robyn?"

"Robyn's with Jaime. Maryjo called," Dad said.

"What did you tell them?"

"The same as I told Davida—that you'd had an accident, that you'd broken your arm."

"That's all?"

Dad squeezed my good hand. "One arm's all that's broken, isn't it?"

"Thanks, Daddy," I said, blinking back tears. Maybe he cared more about my feelings than it had sounded like earlier.

"What time is it?" I asked after a little while, wishing my parents would go so I could be alone.

When they finally did, I immediately wished they were back again.

Marcus-Keeton Hospital at night was not like the hospitals you see on TV. After the lights in my room were out and the hall lights dimmed, it got eerie quiet. The night sounds began—murmuring voices, thumping carts, an old man coughing, then crying and swearing, doors opening and closing, plastic pans dropping—all were sounds I recognized. But what about the strange shufflings and swishings? And who or what sounded like a giant breathing outside my door?

I was acquainted with only two people who worked at Marcus-Keeton and I hadn't seen either one of them. Chances were strong that not a single hospital employee would know Floyd Conner if they saw him. What if he'd heard that all the sirens or had listened to the evening news and guessed where I was? Supposing he was out there someplace, biding his time, waiting for the night to darken so he could sneak in after me?

Hands clammy, I stared till my eyes hurt at the oblong of light shining through the slightly open doorway. After what seemed like hours, I heard footsteps and the door swung slowly open. Terrified, I clutched the edge of the sheet.

"Are you having trouble sleeping, Dear?" asked a soft-voiced nurse. She switched on a small light and checked my vital signs. Then she straightened my tangled covers and wiped my sweaty forehead with a tissue.

"You're afraid, aren't you?"

I opened my mouth to answer and no sound came out.

She said, "Don't worry, Dear. We're all taking special care of you tonight. We know what happened and we're all sorry—so sorry. Sit tight, Honey. I'll be right back."

As she bustled out, I moaned. Obviously the whole world knew and had discussed my stupidity.

The nurse returned and handed me a tiny plastic cup containing a single white pill. "To help you sleep," she explained.

After that I slept. I also dreamed—great, horrid dreams in which I never stopped running from a person or monster I could never quite see.

I awoke next morning exhausted and relieved to see the sun shining through the slits in the blinds as if everything were normal. I'd had a few hard-to-swallow bites of soggy toast before a skinny young man in a white T-shirt and baggy pants strode into my room as if he had a perfect right.

"I'm Dr. Madden and you're Pippa—what an interesting name," he said as he plugged both ears with the stethoscope dangling from his deeply tanned neck.

I glanced beyond him through the open doorway. "Where's Dr. Thorpe? Dr. Thorpe is my doctor," I insisted as I fought to still my panic over having a strange man in my room.

If Dr. Madden was truly a doctor, he sure didn't look the part. His yellowish hair was long in back and his T-shirt looked as if it had dried in a heap instead of being tumbled in a dryer.

As he moved toward the bed my eyes clouded, and I saw only the shadowy form of Floyd Conner towering over me.

"Get away! Don't touch me!" I screeched.

A gray-haired nurse appeared almost instantly. "Shhh. Dr. Thorpe will be in later," she soothed. "Dr. Madden is an intern. He's learning to be a doctor." She paused and winked at him. "He's a practical joker and a flirt, but you have my word, you can trust him."

I felt silly. So silly I was glad she stayed until after Dr. Madden had finished examining me.

He removed the stethoscope from his ears. "How'd you happen to get lucky enough to have a name hung on you like Pippa?"

"My mom read it in a book and liked it."

"Your mom must be some romantic lady. I figured as

good as you are at screeching maybe they'd named you after Pippi Longstockings."

I was beginning to like Dr. Madden. "No, but Dad used to call me that sometimes just to tease her."

Dad walked briskly in around 10:30 and handed me a manila envelope stuffed with polaroid pictures. "They're not just of my office personnel," he said. "There's a picture of every single person who works in the building, including the mailman and the girl who delivers United Parcel. Examine them with care, P.J., then tell me which one is Floyd Conner."

"These are mostly of women," I said as I looked closely at each picture.

"People do disguise themselves."

"Dad—not that creep. I'm positive. He was a man."

Dad watched as the pile of rejects grew.

"No one here even resembles him," I said at last.

"You're sure?"

"I'm sure," I said. trying to shove the pictures back in the envelope, succeeding only in scattering them.

"Here, I'll do that," Dad offered.

I let him. Doing things with a broken arm was going to be more than a little bit awkward.

"I'm relieved," Dad said as he scooped up the pictures. "On the other hand, it would have made identification easier." His mouth smiled; the rest of his face looked grim.

"Daddy?"

"Yes?"

"I—didn't want it to be someone we—you know."

"Right," he said with a sigh.

Dad came back later that afternoon and took me home. He got me in and settled, then he said, "I'm up to my ears at the office. Your mother will be home in less than two hours. She made arrangements for Jaime to get off the bus at Robyn's. They'll bring her home when it's time for Robyn's piano lesson. Do you think you can handle being alone for that long?"

"No problem," I said. What was there to be afraid of in my own house?

"You're sure? Because I can stay—"

"Dad, I know how busy you are. Just go. I'll be fine."

He had scarcely left the driveway before I began hearing noises I had never noticed before. I went to the kitchen for a drink of water and jumped when the refrigerator started. Moments later when the afternoon mail dropped through the front door slot I nearly landed on the ceiling. When the doorbell rang, I practically came unglued.

It rang a second time and a third.

Tiptoeing out into the entry, I peeked through the one bit of clear glass in our leaded iris door window. My knees buckled with relief as I recognized Marvin Bishop, who was retired and lived across the street.

I answered his questions about my arm, touched the garage door opener button so he could locate the pipe wrench he'd come to borrow, and felt considerably better having been reminded that both he and Mrs. Bishop were across the street.

When Maryjo stopped by on her way home from school, I recognized our special signal: two knocks and one short jingle. When I let her in, instead of beginning with school chatter, she looked at me with those big violet eyes, flung her arms around me, and burst into tears.

"P.J., we couldn't imagine what happened yesterday. What did happen?" she asked, as she finished blowing her nose.

"Dad said you called. Didn't he tell you?"

"Not really—except that you'd broken your arm and were in the hospital. I'd've come to visit you, but he said no visitors. How come?" she asked, shrugging out of her heavy coat.

"Dad didn't tell you how stupid I was?" I asked after we were seated together on the couch.

Under normal circumstances a question like that and I'd have been fair game for Maryjo's unique, off-the-wall brand of teasing. This time she flipped the single thick black braid I liked so much over her shoulder and looked solemnly at me.

"We've been friends forever, Pip. You may be impulsive sometimes, but you're not stupid. And even if you were, I'd still be your friend. The radio was on in the kitchen this morning. I heard the news. More happened than just a broken arm. Want to talk about it?"

"Maybe—but just to you. Promise you won't tell?"

Maryjo hesitated. "I'm not sure I should make that kind of promise but—OK, I promise," she said.

I glanced at the clock. Unless Mom decided to come home early, we had plenty of time to talk.

"I was on my way to the mall to meet you and Robyn. It was really cold and sleeting," I began. Without leaving out anything, I told Maryjo everything I could recall about Floyd Conner and all that had happened inside the van and at the park.

6

"Oh, P.J.—" Maryjo's eyes had darkened noticeably with the pain of what I had just told her.

"You're the only person I've told—everything," I said.

"Shouldn't you tell your parents? And the police."

"No! And don't you forget, you promised!"

"Why don't you want them to know?" Maryjo asked.

"Why? Maryjo, do you think I want the whole world calling me stupid for the rest of my life? Besides, I'd die if I had to say stuff like that to a policeman."

"You've said yourself you can talk to your mom about anything," Maryjo retorted. "Maybe if you told her—besides, if no one knows how bad it really was, maybe they won't try very hard to catch him," Maryjo reasoned.

Our conversation was not going the way I had planned. I

got up and went to the window, nursing my arm, staring out at the bank of dark clouds hanging over the neat rows of houses behind ours.

While what she'd said made sense, I so longed to forget the whole episode, to simply blot Floyd Conner out of my life and my mind, I turned and flared, "Maryjo, I am not telling! And if you really want to keep on being my friend, you'd better not either."

"OK," she said, "but you might think about this. If they don't catch him, how will you feel when you find out he's hurt someone else?"

I had started to cry, and now I couldn't make myself stop.

"OK, OK, I'll think about it," I sniffed. Then, as I heard the muffled sound of a car door slamming, "That must be Jaime. Please—will you let her in and keep her occupied while I go wash my face?"

"Can you manage with one hand?"

"Well enough to dry tears," I told her.

My eyes were so red I stayed in the bathroom for a long time. As I leaned over the sink and held a drippy cold washcloth tight against my eyes, I prayed I would have the courage to do whatever was right. By the time I quit washing and got out, Maryjo said it was past time for her to go home. As for all my face washing, I could as well have skipped it.

Jaime took one look when I sauntered into the family room and said, "You've been crying. Does your arm hurt much?"

"Not much now. It hurt really bad at first," I told her.

Her eyes widened. "If it doesn't hurt, then how come you're crying?"

"I'm not, not now. Why don't you go jump rope?" I suggested, naming her favorite pastime.

"Good idea," Jaime said. Flashing me a grin, she snatched a purple nylon jump rope from a chair back and began skipping away in the open space before the fireplace.

Watching her, I thought she looked really cute with her short hair flying out in little sand-colored wings. A barrette hit the hearth and then another. She still had plenty left. Jaime never did anything on a small scale. She was both barrette and jump rope crazy.

Did Floyd Conner know I had a little sister? What if she should happen to be outdoors or walking home from her friend's house alone? What if—

"Jaime, would you like to help me make cookies? I don't think I can manage with just one hand."

"Sure," Jaime replied, using her most grown-up voice.

Perhaps if I did something nice with Jaime and for Mom, the sick feeling in my stomach would go away.

The doctor wanted me to stay home for a few days before going back to school, so it looked as if I'd have to spend the next day alone. Dad came home for lunch, however, and then our youth director called and asked could she come by for a visit with me at 1:30. If I was lucky, maybe she'd stay until Jaime came home from school.

Gwen Sorensen was one of my favorite people. After Dad left, I listened until I heard the whir of her yellow VW Rabbit turning into the driveway and waited for her to ring the doorbell before opening the door. Already I was learning to anticipate sounds so I'd not have any scary surprises.

"You got your hair cut," I said as she stepped inside.

"And you got your arm broken. How is it? And how are you?" Gwen asked, touching my cast with a chubby forefinger. Gwen herself wasn't chubby, but her face and hands and legs looked as if they belonged to someone who was.

I invited her into the family room and we sat down. Gwen apologized for not coming to see me in the hospital. "By the time I discovered you were there, you'd been released," she explained.

"I wasn't feeling much like company anyhow," I said.

Gwen's eyes were a peculiar aquarium green. When she looked directly at you, you felt compelled to look back.

"What happened anyhow?" she asked.

I studied my fingernails. "Not much."

"I have this special mouth," she said. "I can disconnect it completely from my ears. If there is anything you need or want to share, I promise you, it will be our conversation and no one else's."

My insides churned. How much did Gwen already know? Although I was sure I could trust her with my deepest hurts, I chose to play it safe.

"Thanks, but I'm OK and my arm will be too—eventually. Could we please talk about something else?"

"Sure."

"I'll fix a snack."

Gwen groaned. "Please, no food."

"Not even a few Bugles?"

"Bugles? My favorite!" she exclaimed. "Where did you find them? Never mind. I can't afford 99 boxes and that's what I'd buy if I knew where to get Bugles."

When it came to snacks and junk food, Gwen was worse than any of the fifty or so kids in our youth group.

"Mom got them at Thriftway," I said. "At least I think so. It's where she grocery shops."

We crunched until half a bowlful had disappeared into Gwen's special mouth and the rest into my not-so-special one.

Gwen said, "I was wondering about tomorrow afternoon. Do you want to go ahead as planned with the meeting?"

She was speaking of a committee to begin planning February's overnighter.

"Oops. I forgot all about it."

"Want me to change the date? Or shall I have the rest go ahead? They could probably meet at Robyn's."

It took me a scant moment to decide. It might be all right to have something besides my own troubles to think about. "I'll go ahead with it," I said. "Having Maryjo and Robyn won't be like having a committee of kids I don't know too well. They're my best friends. They're here half the time anyhow."

"I can't come, remember," Gwen reminded.

I grinned. "That means we can do as we please."

Gwen made a face. "It all depends on what you please."

I heaved an exaggerated sigh. "You know me. We'll kick around all our wildest ideas and end up doing whatever's allowed."

Later on, as Gwen was leaving, Jaime's bus stopped at the corner. Seeing Gwen, Jaime ran to her and hugged her. Then she walked right on past me and into the house as if I were a part of the door frame. But then I didn't often remember to hug Jaime. Gwen always did.

"Is tonight the night Davida comes to sleep over?" Jaime wanted to know as I closed the door.

Another oops. Although Davida's parents had made arrangements some time ago, I had completely forgotten. Davida had stayed with us off and on while her parents attended out-of-town seminars ever since we'd lived next door to them. We were used to having her. Still, I wasn't sure if I was ready yet for Davida.

"Is she coming?" Jaime asked again.

"We'll see. Now why don't you go jump rope? I've been talking all afternoon and I'm tired." I had just started to realize how tired.

"You haven't been talking to me," Jaime accused.

"Go jump rope for a while and then I will," I promised. Going into the living room, I cradled my cast in a soft pillow and laid down on the sofa.

As I listened to the rhythmic thumping of the purple rope,

the weird voice of Floyd Conner echoed inside my head. I stared up at the ceiling, not wanting even to think about him. Davida either, for that matter. I wanted to think about my friends and to anticipate the fun we'd have together as we planned food and activities for the overnighter.

I must have dozed off because I suddenly found myself running, this time toward Jaime, who stood waiting for her school bus. Behind me I could heard the crunching of feet against gravel. The harsh rasp of heavy breathing came closer and closer to my ear.

I awoke with a start. The house was still. Too still. My heart started to thud. I sat up and looked around. Where was Jaime? Why wasn't she in front of the fireplace jumping rope like usual?

"Jaime?" I called, rushing through the kitchen and into the hall. Then, more frantically, "Jaime!"

"I'm in the bathroom."

Knees weak, I spoke more sharply than I intended. "You don't have to sneak around about it."

The bathroom door opened. "I wasn't. You were asleep. I was being quiet. How come you're all sweaty?"

I lifted my good hand to my forehead. Even my bangs were drenched. I started back to the sofa, then realized. Although Jaime was barely eight, I owed her some kind of explanation.

"I had a scary dream. That's what made me yell at you."

"Was your dream about me?"

I didn't want to frighten her. "Mostly it was about me and breaking my arm. And by the way, you may use the bathroom whenever you like. You don't need my permission."

"Are you sure you can handle having Davida around for two nights?" Mom asked a little while later, after she had gotten home from school and was dumping stuff together for a casserole.

Dad would not be home until late and Jaime had gone to

her room. Davida had a club meeting of some sort and would not be coming until after 9 P.M.

I made a face. "Having Davida around is always a pain."

Mom understood. "I know. What I'm asking is, will two in a bed bother your arm?"

"In my old bed it would have. The waterbed's bigger."

"How about the—other?"

"What other?" I asked, playing dumb.

"Are you apt to feel upset?"

I forced a grin. "If I do, Miss Know-It-All-Junior-Psychiatrist has all the answers."

I sobered. What if I had a nightmare?

Noting my expression, Mom suggested, "Perhaps she could sleep with Jaime this time."

"Davida? She'd hate it. No, Mom, I'll be OK. Honest."

Actually, Davida was like a hot, humid summer day. You could do nothing to change it, so you put up with it and you lived through it. You also knew it was bound to happen again.

About an hour before Davida was to arrive, I asked Mom if she'd come into my room. Dad was on the phone and Jaime was in bed. I had been thinking a lot about what Maryjo had said, and I knew I couldn't risk having Jaime or any other girl hurt because of me.

Mom sat cross-legged on the bed and I sat facing her. We both had on our blue sweats. At the moment, we wore our hair the same, partly because I liked Mom's short page boy and partly because it's how my hair happens to grow. Sometimes Dad called us his twin sisters. We weren't, of course. Mom was 37. She was also lots of fun, but she was strict. I doubted if I could ever be as strict with my kids.

Since there was no easy way to begin, I blurted, "Mom, I think I'd better tell you what really happened Tuesday."

7

Friday was dismal. Sleet rattled against the windows, much as it had the day I had behaved like the stupidest of all ignoramuses.

Inside, the house felt cozy and warm. Mom was home. Due to our private conversation, she had phoned before breakfast and asked for a substitute. Garfield second graders could do without her for one day, she said. I guess she knew how much I needed her.

While she enjoyed a second cup of coffee, I lifted my cast, plopped my other elbow onto the table, and hung my face over a steaming mug of hot chocolate, sniffing appreciatively. Except for the weather, the day should have been perfect.

"How'd your night with Davida go?" Mom asked. "Did you sleep?"

"As good as I ever do with Davida. She's not used to sharing."

Neither was I, since I'd always had a room to myself. Still, there are different ways of looking out for Number One. Davida's seemed more piggish. Perhaps she felt the same about me.

"Any more bad dreams?"

"Where would I get time to dream? Davida hogged the covers like always. I woke up every time she turned over. I'm glad she had to go to school today."

Mom smiled. "Your day's coming, probably about Monday." When I wrinkled my nose, she said, "You can't skip school forever, you know. But you're right about Davida. We don't need anyone extra around today."

"I wish I didn't have to talk to them." By them, I meant the police.

"It has to be done."

"I know. Mom, what will I say? I prayed last night that they'd send a police*woman*. They won't, I know. Mom, it was hard last night saying that stuff to you."

Mom patted my hand. "Just answer their questions, Honey."

Police Chief Myron Gage had a face like the bulldog motif on my cousin Pam's cheerleading sweatshirt. His freckled hands looked as if they belonged to the Pillsbury Doughboy. When Mom offered him a chair and he sat down, the chair creaked and his stomach made big scallops between the buttons of his uniform. I soon discovered he only looked like a grouch.

"School getting along all right without you?" he asked with a friendly grin.

"I doubt if they even miss me," I said. While I had lots of neat friends, I wasn't especially popular.

He asked what I liked best about school. When I said, "Art class," he looked thoughtful.

"Could be useful," he said.

I figured he meant as a career. "I hope so." I said shyly.

He got down to business. "I'm pleased to hear you're prepared to give us more information. Frankly, we're baffled."

I don't know what I'd expected. I suppose I thought he'd scold me for holding back evidence. His unexpected kindness triggered quick tears.

Brushing them away, I said, "There's still a lot I don't remember, but I'll do my best to answer your questions."

His questions were straight and to the point. "The boys said they thought you'd been raped. Were you?"

"No."

"Did anything occur that might lead you to believe that was the man's intent?"

Speaking softly, not looking at him. I told him about the touching and the verbal insults.

"Anything else?"

The horrible memories were like poisonous bats. This time my voice was barely audible. "His clothes were—undone."

Chief Gage's eyes narrowed. He looked at Mom. "Don't worry, we'll catch him," he said.

Mom's face was chalky and she looked all pinchy around her usually happy mouth. "I hope so."

The gist of the questions changed. Now Chief Gage wanted me to describe Floyd Conner.

"I can't," I said. It was the truth.

"We're in no hurry," he coaxed. "Relax. Close your eyes. Get up and go elsewhere if you need to—do whatever it takes to help you remember."

I tried every suggestion. I also plugged my ears to shut out the sounds of Mom and him talking. Nothing worked. All I could see when I thought about Floyd Conner was a lip-licking, nose-first kind of face, like those you saw on the antacid commercials.

The questioning began again.

"Hair? Mustache? Eyebrows?"

"He was kinda old. He had gray hair."

Chief Gage grinned. "Hey, so do I and I'm not old—not yet anyhow."

That was a matter of opinion.

"Eyebrows?"

"Uh—reddish, I think. Bushy—yes, they were bushy—I think." I covered my eyes with my good hand. "Oh, I really don't remember. I can't think—"

"Reddish? That's odd." He stared out the window, at the same time tapping on his pad with a stubby pencil.

He pondered that for a moment. Then he asked, "Pippa, how good are you at drawing pictures of people?"

"I can do caricatures—cartoons—pretty good." Actually, my teacher said I was a whole lot better than good.

"How about drawing me a picture? Not right now. Take your time. Think about your abductor for a while. Then draw us a picture. Include anything and everything you can recall. Think you can handle that?"

The drawing, yes. The thinking about him, no. Aloud, I said, "I'll try. How soon do you want it?"

"Yesterday. No, last Tuesday," he said with a grin meant to show me he was kidding. "Don't worry about it. Of course we'd like to have it, and the sooner the better. But believe me, we understand. You can only do what you can do. Trouble is, the rounder could be three states away while we fool around getting our act together."

"There now, that wasn't so bad, was it?" Mom asked a little while later, after she had closed the door behind Chief Gage.

My stomach felt stuffed with scratchy, squiggly raw noodles. One thing was obvious. Mom had never ever had a man like Floyd Conner mess up her life. Chief Gage knew more about how I felt than she did, and he was a man. Old and obese at that.

For lunch we had my favorite, tuna crunch salad. It had potato chips in it and shredded cabbage and almonds and I don't know what all else. Mom warmed ready-made rolls from the freezer and we had raspberry sorbet and Girl Scout cookies for dessert. It was like an elegant, downtown lunch and I told Mom so.

She looked pleased. "Do you realize we hardly ever do anything together, just you and I?"

I yearned for those warm fuzzy moments to last and last. While it was true that Mom was busy and had hardly any time for frills, she was almost always around when I needed her. Plus, she was a whole lot more fun than most of my friends' mothers. Still, I couldn't help but think about the fact that if I hadn't had a bad experience, the fancy lunch would probably never have happened.

We cleared the table together and then Mom said perhaps I should spend some quiet time in my room thinking about the picture Chief Gage had asked me to draw. Since MacArthur let out at 2:40, I begged off. My friends would be coming soon for the committee meeting and my room was a disaster.

"Need some help?" Mom asked.

"It's hard to hang up clothes with one hand. And my bed's not made."

As she started to help make the bed, Mom pushed a white plastic bag from beneath one corner. "What's this?" she asked.

"The bag's from the hospital. It's the stuff I had on the day—Mom, I don't ever want to see any of those clothes again."

She was already rummaging through the bag. "Honey, it's your new sweater—and your good corduroy slacks."

"Give them to Goodwill."

"You'll get over feeling this way. Then you'll want them."

"No I won't, not ever."

She stuffed the clothes back in the bag and was gone for a moment. Probably she would wash them and put them away until she'd figured I'd forgotten, then try to get me to wear them again. I already knew it was going to be impossible. When she returned and said something silly, although I knew she was doing it on purpose to cheer me up, I decided to let the matter drop.

Mom seldom had time to do chores with me. In spite of the bad start, we ended up having fun.

We also had my room back in order in almost no time. Our house was practically new, so it was fun to keep it looking nice. Easy, too.

When we moved in, Jaime got my old bedroom furniture and I got my new waterbed. I also got to pick a new color scheme. I hoped I wasn't going to get tired of peach and green and black on white. Those colors seemed sophisticated when I chose them, but I still liked blue best. I'd had blue since I was a baby. Probably the folks assumed their first would automatically be a boy. Jaime may also have disappointed them, though neither one ever acted as if it bothered them having two girls.

Mom stood in the doorway. "I've been thinking," she said.

"Did it hurt much?" I asked, still feeling close and more like joking around than I had for days.

"Nope. Didn't leave any scars either," Mom said, smiling, touching the top of her head. "Would you mind—after the girls get here, that is—since I'm home anyhow, maybe I could shop for groceries today and not have to do it tomorrow. Of course that would mean you'd be responsible for Jaime the same as usual, though probably not for long. My grocery list is short this week."

"You know, Mom, you're breaking one of your own rules," I teased.

Our rules for after school were like my first batch of homemade gingersnaps—practically unbreakable. Jaime and I hardly ever got to have anyone over, and if we did ask someone to come over, it had to be one friend at a time. Inviting several kids was never allowed. We didn't go places either, at least not often. I babysat Jaime, practiced piano, and did my homework. After I'd explained who all was involved and why after school was the only time our committee could meet, Mom had finally agreed to let Robyn and Maryjo come over. Davida, too, of course, since we were stuck with her until that evening.

"Just don't get to talking and forget you're looking after Jaime," Mom reminded later, on her way out the door.

I sucked in my breath. When I was in sixth and Jaime in kindergarten, she had repeatedly locked herself in the john. The next year she ground one of our every day spoons into the garbage disposal, which she was never supposed to ever turn on. However, a good hard pinch, brought on by snitching chocolate chips and closing a drawer too fast, had been her only injury during the two and a half years I'd been in charge.

Obviously, in spite of all that had transpired that day, Mom too considered me stupid and irresponsible.

I let my breath out slowly. "Sure, Mom."

8

Maryjo and Robyn arrived on schedule. Half an hour later, Davida straggled in.

By the time Jaime got off her bus, we had armed ourselves with a bag of Cheetos and the rest of the Bugles and were sitting in a circle on my bed. While the committee planned for the overnighter, Davida eyeballed herself in the mirror. Over the murmur of the TV, the slap-slapping of Jaime's jump rope kept me reminded that she was where she belonged.

"Does she have to do that all the time?" Davida asked.

Davida had a beautiful face and a so-so body. The rest of her was what I'd call spoiled rotten. Two days and one night of her was about all I could stand, especially the way things had turned out. Twice a year, whenever her folks attended a really big conference, her stay lasted for a week. I was glad this wasn't one of those times.

"Do what?" I asked, my mind on hoagie fixings. "You mean Jaime? Until Dad gets home. He can't stand it for very long."

"Grief. How can you?" This from Robyn, whose siblings were many and all still in grade school.

I shrugged. "If she's jumping rope and watching *Duck Tales* I don't have to worry. Besides, she's not bugging me any. Doing what she enjoys most is what keeps her from being a pain."

"Games, devotions, food—are we finished. Pippa?" Maryjo asked. Then, before I'd had time to answer, "Davida, what's it like going out with boys?" Maryjo could hardly wait.

Davida's birthday was a scant month before mine, but she looked like she was in college. She smiled a dreamy, secret smile.

"It's all right."

"Dummy. I know it's all right." My water bed rippled beneath the force of Maryjo's anticipation. "What's it like to kiss?"

Three-fourths of our classmates started going out in fifth grade. For many of them, kissing was kid stuff. The rest of us stuck together because of parents who said (1) eighth grade was too young for dating and (2) that the present was our appointed time to continue our education. We could be with the opposite sex as much as we wanted, but only for group activities.

"I don't kiss every boy I go out with," Davida informed us. Rummaging in an initialed overnight case, she drew out a brush and applied it slowly to a mass of tawny hair. "First our minds would have to meet," she said, sounding super serious.

Her dramatics were too much. Maryjo and I leaned forward and zonked heads.

"Like this?" Maryjo asked, and Robyn collapsed in a fit of wild giggling.

Cramming the picture of Floyd Conner's slobbering mouth as deep down as my memory would allow, I moaned. "I won't be able to kiss, not in a hundred years."

All eyes swiveled toward me.

"How come?" Robyn wanted to know.

I tapped my braces. "Who'd want to kiss with *these*?"

In my mind, I conjured up a photo I'd once seen of two buck deer whose antlers got locked together during a fight. They starved to death like that. For me to kiss anyone other than Oren was unthinkable, and Oren too had braces.

The committee notes were still on my lap. My thoughts went into automatic pilot as I filled the empty space at the bottom of the page by writing Oren Donald Richardson as many ways as I could think of.

"Lookit. O.D.R. Oder. Like in Phew!" Maryjo said, grabbing the paper, waving it for the rest to see.

She gave it back right away. "Just kidding, P.J. Oren's neat. If you didn't like him, I would."

Now that's what I'd call loyalty.

"I might kiss, but I'm not touching. Mom says that's what gets girls in trouble." Robyn said, and added, "With four kids, she'd ought to know."

My teeth clenched together so hard my ears ached. I shut my eyes and tried hard not to shudder visibly. With a great deal of effort, I forced myself to ignore what I was feeling inside so I could keep on having fun.

Before Oren, kissing conversations had been of no interest to me. Going further with a boy was not even an option. Mom said my face was like a baby's first picture book, meaning she could guess what was on my mind almost before I knew myself. Now I wondered. Could my friends tell by looking at my face that I'd thought some lately about what it might be like to kiss Oren? Worse yet, could

Robyn and Maryjo, my two very best friends, tell that part of me was only pretending to enjoy the conversation? Maryjo knew, of course, about Floyd Conner and his fat, slobbering lips.

As if she had read my mind, Maryjo glanced quietly at me. "Want me to change the subject?" she mouthed while Davida was saying something to Robyn.

"I'm OK." I mouthed back.

Aloud, I quipped, "I'm not touching until after I'm married and have two kids." Even to my own ears, my voice came out sounding loud and unnatural.

Maryjo and Robyn lapsed into another fit of laughing. Davida eyed me with disdain. "Pippa, you are so naive."

Maybe so. But I got better grades than she did and I sure as the world had more friends. Since she was a guest in our home, I kept my big mouth shut. If I'd had my say, Davida wouldn't have stayed with us every time her folks traipsed off to wherever it was they went for their dumb old meetings.

A few minutes later when Mom came in with the groceries and announced that Davida's parents had returned, I didn't shed a tear. I don't suppose Davida did either.

After Davida finally got all her stuff gathered together and left, I glanced at my black-and-white cat clock. "You two will have to vamoose in fifteen minutes," I said. "We eat early on Fridays. Dad bowls in his league even during tax season."

Actually, we almost always ate out or ordered in on Fridays because Mom liked celebrating at the end of a busy, happy, productive week. Mostly, if Dad bowled, we ordered in so he'd be sure to make it to Tipenny Lanes by seven.

"Lucky," Robyn said as she was leaving and had just found out we had pizza coming at 5:45.

She moaned. "We'll probably have leftovers. Mom's always out of food by the end of the week." She pulled a bright stocking cap over her short perm and giggled. "Maybe she's making leftovers pizza."

"Yuk," I said as I let her out the door. My smile vanished the moment she had gone. But for a few hours, thanks to my friends, my life had been practically normal. Maybe I too had something to celebrate.

"Paper plates tonight, Jaime, and we'll drink our soda from the cans. No dishes—and we'll have five extra minutes for shopping," Mom was saying as I returned to the kitchen.

Shopping?

I swallowed. We almost always shopped on Friday nights while Dad bowled. Sticking to a schedule was how Mom kept up.

"I can't go shopping with my arm like this," I said after a little while.

Mom arranged veggies on a paper plate and set them on the table. Mom could make even a table set with paper plates look elegant.

Glancing to make sure Jaime was out of earshot, she said, "Pippa, I've not only planned to go, I need to go. You're welcome to stay home, but you know Jaime. She won't want to. Are you ready to be in the house alone at night? Think it over."

Thinking it over took maybe ten seconds.

"May I buy that sweater. the one I showed you last time?" I asked. Instead of paying me for babysitting Jaime, the folks gave me a small allowance. In addition, I got to buy something I wanted or needed about once a month. Usually I bought clothes.

"I'm getting new barrettes—with ribbons." Jaime announced as we discussed the sweater.

Later on at the mall, although barrettes literally dripped off her hair already, we shopped for Jaime first. When I objected, Mom said it was not spoiling her, that she was simply being practical. She was right. The minute Jaime had her little white bag in hand, she stopped bugging Mom and behaved herself.

Trying on a sweater over a cast was a hassle. It looked super on me so I bought it. Mom got the stuff she needed and then we window shopped until time to leave for the bowling alley. We had two cars, but we almost always went places together on Friday nights because we liked doing fun things after shopping and bowling.

At dinner, while we were scarfing up the last of the pizza, Dad had winked at Mom and suggested, "We'd better go have some more ice cream after a while. Pippa's like you, Freda—getting lovelier every day. Next thing we know the boys will be hanging around and they'll be buying her more ice cream than she can eat."

"Oh, Dad," I said, though not as vehemently as I used to before I started noticing Oren.

So the plans were to go for ice cream.

While I had hesitated over going to the mall, the lights there had been bright and the shoppers mostly families or couples out having a good time. It went far better than I'd anticipated.

Tipenny Lanes, except for over the lanes, was dimly lit. It was noisy and smoky and filled mostly with men. As we entered, I moved closer to Mom and stayed there.

Dad had finished and was changing into street shoes. In reply to questions about my cast, he said I'd had a little accident, then changed the subject by bragging to his colleagues about Jaime's outstanding reading ability.

"This one," he boasted, putting an arm around my good shoulder, "is an artist."

"My wife works with oils. What interests you?" a friend of Dad's was asking when suddenly I froze.

The man holding the ball two alleys away looked like Floyd Conner! It couldn't be, of course. Floyd had gray hair and he'd been much older. Except for a rim of rabbit-colored hair in back and a frizzy puff jutting over his forehead, this man's head was as slick and as white as my grandma's old vinegar cruet. Weird.

Still fighting panic, I spread my mouth into what I hoped was a presentable smile. "We haven't done oils yet—at school, I mean. I enjoy water color. Cartooning is my favorite."

"A new Al Capp, eh?"

I couldn't help myself—my eyes were drawn to the man across the room. He'd just made a strike and was grinning all over his face. Floyd Conner had never looked that ordinary or that pleasant, not to me. It couldn't possibly be the same man.

"Excuse me," I said. "I couldn't think for a minute who Al Capp was."

"He drew Li'l Abner. I guess Capp was before your time."

"I'm more the Charles Schulz type," I said, hoping it was true.

Jaime was swinging on Dad's arm, begging. "Can we go to the Dairy Queen?"

"I don't know—may we?" Dad teased.

At the DQ, Dad pointed out a sign. Peanut Buster Parfaits were on sale for the rest of the month. My favorite under normal circumstances.

"I'm not very hungry. I'll have a Dilly Bar," I told him.

A Dilly Bar was the smallest item you could order. While the rest pigged out on peanuts dripping with chocolate syrup, I nibbled at the waxy chocolate coating. When I was nearly half through eating it, a big piece of chocolate fell off, revealing a rounded edge of white ice cream.

I stopped nibbling and stared at it. As it started to melt, the shiny ice cream shimmered briefly like the white, white skin of that grinning bowler's face. He still reminded me of Floyd Conner. My stomach heaved.

Grabbing a fistful of napkins from the dispenser, I wadded

the rest of the treat inside them and got up and threw it down into the dark recesses of a nearby trash container.

Fighting back tears of frustration, I walked slowly back to the booth and sat down.

If I never again enjoyed the special taste of a Dilly Bar, it would forever be Floyd Conner's fault.

9

Next morning, Dad drove off to work at his usual time. He almost always worked Saturdays during tax season. A light snow had fallen during the night, and Jaime was eager to finish her chores so she could play outside. She was in the bathroom cleaning the sink.

"Do I have to go to church tomorrow?" I asked Mom.

Mom wiped up the syrup spills around Jaime's place at the table. She sighed. "Life goes on, Pippa. You can't avoid people."

"Does it have to go on tomorrow?"

Mom had tried hard all along to be understanding. "Honey, I know being at Tipenny's last night upset you. It was dark in there—and so many strangers, nearly all of them men. I can see why."

No you can't, not really, because I never said a word about that bald-headed guy in the next lane looking like Floyd Conner.

"Church will be different," she assured me.

I shook my head. "Everybody will stare at me."

"I doubt that."

"They'll ask questions."

Mom pondered for a moment. "May I make a suggestion?" she asked.

"Good or bad?"

"Good, of course."

"It better be. My face is still a mess. I look awful."

"Your friends won't mind," she said. "We could invite a few of them over this evening and—"

"Mom!"

"Wait, hear me out," she said.

When we studied the fruits of the Spirit in Sunday school, patience was not my best subject. I lifted my arms, intending to cross them over my chest while I heard her out. It didn't work too well. At best I probably resembled the bargain turkeys Mom bought for a lower price because one wing was broken or missing.

"Besides being more comfortable around your closest friends, you could answer their questions right here at home. If you let them know you don't enjoy being in the spotlight, they might be the very ones to surround you in the morning and answer those questions for you."

"Do you think so?"

"Don't most people enjoy being in the know?" she said, and added, "It might help to remember that only a few of us know anything about what might be hardest to talk about. Answering questions may turn out to be easier than you think."

Her prediction could have come true if I hadn't included Davida. Since she didn't go to church, I almost always invited her if I had a group of church kids over. While she wasn't my favorite person, I really cared about the fact that she was missing out on the neatest way there is to live because she wasn't a Christian. Sometimes she came, sometimes not. We decided on six other kids besides Maryjo and Robyn.

Davida not only came, she took over.

The kids wrote crazy stuff on my cast and autographed it. We watched a funny video and ate and laughed and talked. A few asked questions. I said I was stupid to get in a van when I knew better and they accepted the statement at face value. When I asked could we change the subject, they all said sure.

Not Davida.

"You know what I think," she said shortly after the subject had been dropped. Without waiting for anyone's go ahead, she talked on. "I think most people get themselves into hairy situations by asking for it. For instance, how were you walking that day, Pippa? Did you stare boldly from the sidewalk at the men passing by in the traffic? Did you flirt with that man, what's-his-name, just a little bit? I'm curious."

Maryjo frowned at her. "Drop it, Davida."

Davida gave her a look. "How *were* you walking, P.J.?"

"With my head down. It was sleeting. The wind was blowing. It was cold."

"Maybe you had on too much makeup—a sure sign of a come-on."

"Davida, that's stupid," someone said.

"Besides, I don't wear makeup. It's too much bother."

Davida bulldozed on. "You must have done something or—"

Mom came in and shut off the TV. "I'll tell you what I think," she said. "If we're all going to make it in time for Sunday school, it's time to get home and find your pajamas and teddy bears."

We were used to parents calling time on whatever we did on Saturday nights. Sundays were special and most of us had been taught that we should be at our best for worship. Davida, of course, would laze in bed like usual.

In spite of Maryjo's defense and Mom's intervention, sleep came slowly that night. What if I had been sending out signals? How was a person to know if she was or wasn't? Just thinking about what Davida had said made me toss and turn for what seemed like hours.

The next morning a chorus of army buglers might have been helpful when it was time to get up and get ready for church. In fact, I'd swallowed quite a bit of orange juice and consumed half a cinnamon roll before I woke up and realized it was Sunday.

Mom's predictions turned out to be right. Few asked about stuff they'd surely heard on the news. Most commented on the size of my cast and asked how my arm was doing. In class, Gwen prayed for the break to heal quickly and that I might enjoy a good week at school. For a solid two and a half hours I felt warm and secure and loved. Sunday night turned out to be a pleasant repeat. Due to my lack of sleep, I napped for two hours in the afternoon, which about wiped out Sunday.

Monday was the pits.

Dad waited and drove me to school so I wouldn't have to carry all the books Maryjo had brought home so I could keep up with my homework.

I should have walked. Getting to school early after you'd been the topmost subject on TV news was definitely the wrong move.

The few times I had been lucky enough to be at the center of everyone's attention, I had enjoyed it. This was different.

By noon, I was ready to barf if one more student whose name I didn't even know rushed up to me and gushed, "Pippa, how awful! How are you anyhow?" Davida's Saturday night grilling dwindled to a mere unkindness alongside the rudeness of those who wanted graphic descriptions of my encounter with Floyd Conner. Following a lunch period interrupted by collectors of gory details, I fled to the girls' room in tears.

Maryjo followed me in and shut the door. "Why don't you talk to the counselor? She'll make them stop," she suggested as she dampened and squeezed out paper towels so I could wash my face.

"And end up having to tell her the whole sordid story? No thanks," I said.

"I'll go with you. I'll even do the talking," Maryjo offered.

"Maryjo, I'm not going!" I insisted and started crying all over again. This time my tears were for Maryjo. She had been my very closest friend since we were babies and here I was treating her like dirt.

"I hate Floyd Conner and this stupid school and all the dumb kids in it," I stormed. At the moment, I hated anything that forced me to snap at my best friend.

Maryjo refused to let my nasty behavior bother her. She was waiting for me at 2:40 and we walked home together as usual. If she didn't have practice for marching band, Robyn sometimes walked with us. In cold weather, they practiced in the gym.

"I'll bet the teacher goes bananas with all those sour notes blasting away under one roof," Maryjo said as we donned coats and mittens. She had to help me with mine.

We lingered until after almost everyone had gone. Then we left by a side door and started toward home on the sidewalk that cut diagonally across the corner of the campus.

MacArthur faced along Fairview. By taking this route, we

could jog over to Mugheny Street and reach Pepperidge Lane without ever having to walk along Fairview. Given a choice, I wished I would never ever have to walk along Fairview again.

We had barely left the school ground when a vehicle turned off Fairview and moved slowly toward where we were crossing the street.

I clutched at Maryjo. "That van. It's white!" I said in a hoarse whisper. "Quick, get the license number!"

I was hanging onto her so tightly she couldn't have written a digit if both our lives depended on it. Before she could locate a pen, the van had turned again onto a side street where it soon vanished.

Our voices came out in unison as we looked at each other and recited the number. Every digit tallied.

"So we've memorized the number—now what?" Maryjo wanted to know.

I still had ahold of her. "Call the police."

"Then c'mon. We'll use the phone in the school office."

"I'd rather do it at home." I said, not wanting to go back, to bare my frightened self before even more people I hardly knew. I was shaking all over. "Let's run."

Maryjo refused to. "The ground's frozen. You could trip and fall and hurt your arm even worse."

We walked so fast, by the time we were in the house I was so out of breath I had to rest for a minute before I could talk. Even after I'd dialed the police station and been put through to Chief Gage, my voice still came out in panicky little gasps.

"White van," I stammered. "We saw the white van!"

Chief Gage said to calm down, asked about the location, wrote down the license number, said he'd keep us informed, and hung up.

"I'd better call Dad and Mom." I said, chewing off one of the fingernails I'd let grow since Christmas. To quit biting my nails had been my one New Year's resolution. Some resolution. One dumb van and I blew it.

"Why bother your folks? I can stay with you. We can do our homework while we wait," Maryjo suggested. Maryjo had no siblings to look after. As long as she stuck to rules about who and where, and let her parents know, she could do as she liked after school.

"Your parents can't do anything the police aren't already doing," Maryjo went on.

"OK, but don't expect me to do much homework. I'm too upset."

Before we'd had time to open our books, the police called back. The van, they said, belonged to a widow lady who did custom cake decorating. Upholstered with white vinyl for easy cleaning, it was outfitted with special trays and shelves to hold the various parts of her cakes she put together on location. The interior was all white and the van had sliding side panels. Floyd Conner's van had been blue inside with doors that opened in back.

"You'll be all right now that it's overwith," Maryjo comforted when it was time for her to leave for her piano lesson.

Jaime came in and I looked at her school papers and fixed her a snack. Leaving her with the TV and her jump rope, I went to my room and curled up on the bed. Turning back the spread, I located the satin edge of the blanket and rubbed it against my cheek. When I was little, the satin on all my blankets wore out really fast. I'd forgotten how soothing it was to hold onto the soft binding.

I don't know when Jaime turned off the TV or how soon the house got quiet. The first I knew she was in my room was when I felt the bed jiggle and smelled her peanut butter breath.

"Here," she said, leaning over me to press a gray flannel rabbit beneath my cast. "You can hold Bun-Bun." Fashioned by our grandmother, the flop-eared rabbit had inhabited Jaime's crib for months before she was born.

How often had I told Jaime what a dumb name Bun-Bun was for a toy?

Jaime snuggled against my back and flung a chubby arm across my shoulder.

"Thank you, Jaime," I said.

Her sweaty hand patting my face seemed more genuine and was more comforting than all the words I had heard during the last week put together.

We were still there when Mom got home. I didn't have to go to school the next day.

10

A blue 10 adorned Oren's basketball jersey. His long legs, still tan from summer, looked great with white shorts. To me, Oren was a 10 in every way you could name.

He had started to notice me too, which made going to school much easier. Even on days when I didn't feel up to facing anyone else, I still had Oren to look forward to.

I'd known him since seventh grade. I started liking him at the beginning of eighth. I didn't know what got him interested in me. Osmosis maybe. We belonged to different churches or it might have happened sooner.

In the fall, I had noticed right off how Oren didn't hang around with girls a whole lot. Perhaps, being so heavily involved with sports, he was different from other popular guys. Maybe it had to do with his being a part of the churchgoing group. Possibly, he was waiting to get to know me.

Oren and I had one class together, and some days we'd end up at the drinking fountain or lockers at the same time. Twice when that happened, he walked me to class. Then one morning I found a basketball joke taped to my locker with the initials O.R. in the lower right corner. At noon that same day, he swung his long leg over the back of the empty chair beside mine and we ate lunch together. After that he waited for me outside the cafeteria. I still sat with Maryjo and Robyn. Oren didn't care. He liked being with a group.

He also liked for me to be at his after school games. Attending those meant I had to go home at my usual time, wait for Jaime, and argue with her about missing *Duck Tales* and going without her jump rope for one afternoon. Then we'd walk back to the gym in time for the game. Seventh grade played first, otherwise I would not have had time for all that.

The hardest part was wondering what I would do if Floyd Conner happened along while I was between school and home. How would I ever protect Jaime?

So while I watched in all directions, we walked as fast as my clumsy cast would allow (usually until Jaime was out of breathe or complained of a side ache). Once we were inside the gym, I could forget Floyd Conner and yell and stomp and laugh like other kids. Often I wished Oren played basketball every day. He did, of course, but not always for games. While there were girls who hung around the gym every day during practice, Mom would never have allowed me to be one of them.

Before Oren, I could take basketball or leave it. Mostly I'd left it to those who were into sports. I knew very few of the rules. I knew enough to cheer if someone on our team scored a basket. Otherwise I cheered only after the rest of our school had started to yell. Because Oren made baskets so often, I was first to yell quite a bit, so I doubt if anyone noticed.

Oren went to elementary school at Garfield, where Mom taught. She'd had him in second grade. Even then, he was tallest in his class.

On the day we played North, our biggest rival from the other side of town, the teams were so evenly matched, the zig-zagging score changed every few seconds. Jaime had begged not to have to go. She hunched beside me with her fingers in her ears, while Maryjo and I watched and yelled and beat each other's backs when MacArthur scored.

Then it happened. With North one point ahead and 19 seconds left in the ball game, Oren risked a long shot and won the game for MacArthur by one point. The crowd went wild. Me first. Oren walked off the floor and wiped his face with a towel as if he'd done nothing spectacular.

By then it was six o'clock and already getting dark. Ignoring the herd of cheerleaders glomming around Oren, I grabbed Jaime's hand and started home. I wasn't worried. One at a time, cheerleaders could be lethal. In loud-mouthed groups of five, they were not much of a threat.

As we left the gym I was so excited over Oren's split-second timing I forgot, for the first time, to keep an eye peeled for Floyd Conner.

Dad pulled into the driveway as we were getting home. On our way into the house, he said, "I hope you're free after school tomorrow, P.J. I could use a little help at the office."

My mouth went dry. "Daddy, I—"

I what? Helping Dad had been one of my favorites for after school. Besides learning new skills, going to the office gave me an occasional break from babysitting. What's more, my funds had gotten low. Dad paid Robyn to babysit Jaime whenever I worked. Robyn hardly ever had much money of her own, so when I worked we both benefited.

"OK," I said. "I'll check with Robyn."

The next day I remembered why I hadn't wanted to go to the office. For starters, I had to walk two blocks down Fairview and cross the street before I could catch a downtown bus. I hadn't walked along Fairview since the day of my great stupidity. I had vowed I would try never to have to do it again. But you do what you have to do.

As it turned out, several of my classmates were going in that direction and some boarded the same bus. When the bus stopped in front of Taco Bell, at the intersection where Floyd Conner had sped away instead of turning, two of them got off with me.

So far, so good, I thought, as I opened the heavy oak door to Dad's building and stepped inside the foyer. Faced with a second dilemma, I stopped.

Dad's accounting firm was on the third floor. Directly before me was an elevator. To my right was an open stairway that became more and more closed as you spiraled upward. Floyd Conner could be lurking in either place. I might never know which one until it was too late.

The brass pendulum of an old school-type clock made kind of a brushing sound as it marked the time. Five minutes passed.

I began to hear other sounds. Typewriters, the ringing of a telephone, a burst of coughing, all came from behind the closed doors leading to the downstairs law offices.

The elevator rippled softly downward and stopped. As the door rumbled open, two men got off. One nodded in my direction as they walked past me and out onto the street.

Should I risk the elevator? Or would I have a better chance of getting away if I chose the stairs. I had to decide.

God, please, I'm so scared!

A woman dressed in a fur coat came in, crossed the narrow lobby and touched the elevator button with a leather-gloved finger.

"Wait," I said, and stepped in after her. The door closed

and for a moment I panicked. What if she turned out to be Floyd Conner in disguise?

I berated myself. What could possibly happen with a thin-faced old woman on an elevator in the thirty seconds required to rise to the third floor?

The woman turned out to be a client of one of Dad's associates. I followed her down the hall as far as Dad's office.

Dad barely looked up. When he finally leaned back in his chair, he asked, "Are you all right?"

"Yeah, why?"

"You're not your usual smiley self. Your eyes look big. Have you had another scare?"

"No," I said in a small voice. How could I say that I had just faced what to me was worse than a firing squad?

Dad was not only perceptive, he was tenacious. "So what's wrong?" he probed.

"I'm being a scaredy cat again, that's all. I know it's stupid to think Floyd Conner could be anywhere in the building—"

Dad's eyes darkened. "He's not here, Honey. You can take my word for it. Don't you remember? I took pictures of everyone who works in the building."

"Right. I remember." Only what if Floyd Conner had found a way to avoid Dad's friend's camera? Suppose he was hiding right now in some dark closet?

"I'd better get to work," I said.

I picked up the gray plastic basket on the corner of Dad's desk. I needed no instructions. Dad's copy work, as well as all the rest, was always carefully marked with little yellow Post-it notes so all I had to do was go down the hall and get started.

Dad's office building was old and narrow. On each floor the hall went down the middle with offices on each side. At the far end on third floor they had taken out partitions to make one big room. Filled with assorted office machines, its walls were lined with file cabinets.

On my way down the hall my head swiveled from side to

side as I glanced through each open doorway. To my relief, at least half of the people behind those big desks were women. Only one of the men had gray hair and he didn't look at all like Floyd Conner. He was much too fat.

As I entered the room with the file basket clutched tightly against my chest, I heard the welcoming click of a printer. I had already met the office girl, who looked up, smiled, and went on working. Hardly anyone had ever worked in there before when I was there. She stayed the whole two hours. Probably Dad had her working in there on purpose.

Although I found it awkward working with mostly one hand, I managed to have everything finished by the time Dad was ready to leave around six.

On the way home, he said, "I could use you about twice a week, maybe even more often, for the next few weeks. Would that fit in with your plans?"

"Fridays, if we have a home game, I like to go."

"That's right. Oren what's-his-name is a basketball player," Dad teased. He grinned. "I promise, no Fridays."

"Daddy, even if Oren wasn't playing, I'd probably want to go."

"Right," he said, still grinning.

"Dad—"

"What, P.J.?"

"Could you come get me from school when you need me to work?"

He frowned. "Honey, if it were any other time of year—"

If only I hadn't had to enter that building alone. Or decide how best to get up to third floor. I swallowed.

Dad could see it was a problem to me. He said, "I wouldn't have time myself. Perhaps I could send someone."

No way, never again.

"Forget it," I said. "I'll be OK."

Surely God would forgive me if it turned out I was not telling the truth.

11

"Cloudy Winterset spoke in art class today," I told everyone one blustery February evening as we lingered together over dinner. Cloudy was our local semi-famous artist. At least "semi-famous" was what she'd called herself in class. "She talked about watercolor. She showed us how to do oceans and waves. That's what she paints most of the time. Some of the kids think they'll do water scenes for spring contest. Not me. I'm not that crazy about doing ships or sand, and you about need one or the other if you do water."

"When is spring contest?" Mom asked.

"Not for ages. I'm not starting until I get inspired."

"Pippa?"

The next subject was not going to be to my liking, I could tell.

"You haven't finished that picture for Chief Gage."

A scowl settled over my face, which had finally healed of all its bruises. "Do we have to talk about that right now?" I asked.

"When *do* you want to talk about it?"

"I don't."

"Have you even tried?" Dad wanted to know.

"Yes, I've tried! I've tried until I'm blue in the face and I just can't. May I be excused?" I asked abruptly.

"Dessert's your favorite," Mom reminded.

"I'm not hungry," I said, fighting against tears.

Mom slid back her chair and came and put her arms around me. "I'm sorry, Honey. I shouldn't have mentioned it at dinner. Please, forgive me."

"You're forgiven," I blubbered, soaking the shoulder of her new cotton sweater with tears I could no longer hold back. "It's just that—sometimes I wish I never had to talk or think about—things—ever again."

"I know," she soothed, patting me.

Jaime got up and went to the kitchen and brought back a fistful of tissues. "Here," she said, looking at first one and then the other of us as if she was about to cry herself.

I wiped my eyes and blew my nose and sat back down. But having to think even briefly about Floyd Conner made the butterscotch pudding stick in my throat.

Mom and Dad were right to keep bugging me. The sooner the police knew what he looked like, the sooner they would catch him and lock him up, and I'd be free to forget the whole mess.

With that in mind, since it was Jaime's turn to help with dishes, I finished eating, went to my room, and got out my drawing supplies.

The gray hair was easy. Thick, stringy, parted off-center with squiggly waves going back. Although the face continued to elude me, I knew it was scary and awful.

One detail I could never forget was the tobacco juice, those yukky brown dribbles filling the lines around his mouth. Or were they wrinkles? With all that gray hair, he had to be wrinkled, didn't he? At last I drew a blank kind of a face and put away my art supplies.

"Here," I said, going out to the living room, dropping the sketch onto the coffee table.

Turning to Dad, I asked. "Where's the paper? I haven't had a chance to look at it yet." Always after Dad finished reading it, he folded it neatly and laid it on the floor beside his chair.

"Paper?" he hedged.

Something in his tone made me forget about the half-finished picture and being a little bit mad at him.

Mom looked up from the magazine she was reading. "Don't you have homework?"

"I'm all caught up, I've practiced one-handed piano, and I did my best with the dumb picture. Where's the paper?"

Mom and Dad exchanged looks. "I—put it out," Dad finally admitted.

"Out" meant an apple box in the garage where we kept papers until we'd collected enough to bundle for recycling. The current edition was on top. The bold letters of a major headline explained why Dad had been so eager to whisk it out of my sight: *Springfield Girl Missing, Feared Abducted.*

Below the headline was a picture of a curly-haired blond who looked about nine or ten years old.

I sat down on the cold cement step and read the story from beginning to end. I don't know when Mom got there, but she was standing in the kitchen doorway behind me when I finished.

Gently touching my shoulder, she said, "Better come back inside and close the door."

Obediently, I laid the paper back in the box. As long as I lived, I would remember the face of that pretty little girl smiling back at me as if she hadn't a care in the world.

"I should have tried harder to draw him." I sobbed. "Then it wouldn't have happened. That little girl—"

"Hush. It's not your fault," Mom said. "That took place in Springfield, not here. Springfield is a hundred miles away."

"He probably drove there in the van."

"In this weather? Don't be silly."

I wasn't being silly. What's more, I could tell by the jiggle in Mom's voice that she wasn't any too sure about Floyd Conner herself.

I returned to my room and tried one more time to do the picture.

"Please, Jesus," I whispered. "If I can't finish this face, and if they don't find that little girl right away, it's going to be all my fault."

At bedtime when Mom came in to say good night I was still fully dressed and doodling across the corner of the art paper.

"Why not forget about it for tonight," she suggested as she retrieved a wad of art paper and stuffed it into my overflowing wastebasket. "Get a good night's sleep and nothing will seem quite as bad in the morning."

While I dressed for bed, Mom folded my sweatshirt and put it away and then brushed my hair like she'd done when I was little.

You'd have thought I was Jaime the way she read to me from my Bible and listened to my prayers and then prayed for me. In spite of the bad evening, for the first time in ages, I fell asleep without first staring into the shadows while my thoughts went wild.

I had a bad dream anyhow.

In it, as in all the others, I ran and ran, fell, scrambled to my feet and ran harder and harder, finally awakening in a cold sweat, too frightened to go back to sleep.

It was the same running dream I'd had before except in

this one I held onto a little girl's hand, dragging her, half-carrying her along with me. The child had a headful of tousled blonde curls. Her face was Jaime's.

"Jaime! Jaime! Run!"

I must have screamed her name aloud, for when I awoke I saw Jaime standing in the small pool of light surrounding my night light.

She rubbed her eyes. "What do you want?" she asked in a sleepy voice.

The door to our parents' room opened and the hall light came on. I must have hollered pretty loud because Dad and Mom were both up. Usually Mom took care of middle-of-the-night problems.

"Another nightmare," Mom said.

Still mute with fright, I nodded.

"You woke me up," Jaime accused.

Dad stooped and hugged her. "Well, we've got the situation under control, so you can snuggle back into your bed and go to sleep."

"But P.J. called me."

My tongue loosened. "That's because you were—" I stopped. "I—you weren't even in my dream, not really. I must not have known what I was doing to call you," I said, avoiding the whole truth. There was no need to frighten Jaime.

Dad tucked her in and closed her door and turned off the hall light. When he came back, we talked in low tones for a few minutes. Mostly my folks prayed and said comforting kinds of things. I didn't tell them my dream or about seeing Jaime's face in it. I didn't want to upset them.

"Since this keeps happening, perhaps we ought to see about counseling." Dad suggested. "Dr. Thorpe thinks it may be a good idea."

I hated the idea of talking to yet another stranger about my problems. "I'll be OK, honest. It's just taking me some time. And anyhow, I've got you two and Gwen and Pastor Henley. You all help me—lots."

Dad tweaked my toe where it stuck up under the covers. "All right for now," he said. "But if these nightmares persist, you get no choice. Fair enough?"

"Fair enough."

"Please stay with me," I begged Mom as they started to go back to bed.

Mine was not the best kind of waterbed for sleeping two. It jiggled a lot. I don't know about Mom. If it bothered her she never said so. She was up next morning, same as usual. So was I, bleary-eyed and grouchy, until I remembered what week it was. Then I got so excited I forgot for a while to worry.

12

Next day after school, Jaime dropped her papers on the table and announced, "I'll be outside."

Melting snow dripped from the eaves and the sidewalks were clear. Earlier, walking home with Maryjo, talking excitedly about the upcoming basketball tournament, I'd wished I'd worn a lighter jacket.

"Oh, no, you won't," I told Jaime.

She stared at me. "Why not?"

"Because you're not. Not today, maybe not ever—at least not while I'm in charge."

A tiny frown flitted across her face, and then she giggled. "Pippa, stop teasing."

"I'm not teasing. I mean it. I want you to stay right here in this house."

"But it's sunshiny."

"What's the matter with you? You never want to play outside. It's almost time for *Duck Tales*," I coaxed.

The frown had turned into a scowl. Jaime opened the door. "I'm going."

"No, you're not."

"Give me one good reason."

Because I'm scared. Scared of last night's dream. Scared of Floyd Conner . . .

"Because I'm in charge and Mom and Dad said you have to mind me."

"They never said I couldn't play outside."

"Look, you'll get all hot and catch cold and it will be my fault for letting you."

"No I won't."

"If you jump rope you will."

"Won't."

"Will. Jaime—"

She closed the door and slouched onto the family room couch.

I said, "If you need anything I'm in my room studying."

She turned on the TV and a moment later shouted above a blaring commercial, "I'm telling Mom!"

Usually Jaime and I got along fine. Fighting with an eight-year-old seemed childish and immature, but there was no way I was going to make it easy for Floyd Conner to snatch away the only little sister I was ever likely to have.

Sunshine beckoned again the next afternoon when Dad phoned to say he needed my help at the office. This time, having to catch a bus on Fairview seemed small by comparison. No matter what I said before I left, Jaime would soon have Robyn talked into allowing her to play outside.

"Daddy?"

"I'm pretty busy."

I swallowed. "Couldn't you get along without me?"

"Why do you think I called you?" he asked.

An idea had started to form. "Dad, I'd have to ask her, but would it be OK if Robyn came instead?"

"Do you have extra homework or someplace else you need to be?" Dad wanted to know.

"No. But Robyn—"

"Someone would have to stop their work and show Robyn what to do," Dad told me. There was sternness in his tone. "P.J., we count on you. You wanted this job, remember? So unless you have some exceptional reason for not coming, I suggest you contact Robyn and then get yourself down here and get to work."

Twenty minutes later I scuttled up the stairs to Dad's office. Dad hadn't exaggerated a bit. Every gray basket in the complex was piled to the brim. Hurrying to get it all done in two hours, I forgot to fret over whether or not Robyn was being too lenient with Jaime. By the time we got home, Robyn had gone and Mom was making dinner. Watching her, I wished as I had so often lately that she didn't have to teach, that she could be there for Jaime and me every day after school.

Then the tournament started and my newest and greatest worry had to do with whether or not MacArthur would win. Surely we would. Oren was the best player our school had seen in years and I wasn't the only person who said so.

Unlike some tournaments, the games took place in several schools. I didn't get to go to any of the preliminaries. But, lucky for me, the final game turned out to be at MacArthur. We made it through to the finals with MacArthur scheduled to play against Central for the championship.

That day the bleacher side of the gym was jampacked by

the time I'd gone home and returned with Jaime in tow. We barely found a seat before the visiting team ran out onto the floor. When our first man came into view, our cheerleaders jumped into action. The crowd went wild. We would win. We had to.

Twice before the game started, Oren looked up at me and smiled. Once the buzzer signaled the start, it was all basketball with him. He never glanced my way again, not even during half time. The crowd shifted some then, so Maryjo came and sat with us.

"Do you think we'll win?" she asked. We were behind by four points.

"Oren's playing. We'll win," I said.

"Central's number 14 is good. Tall, too."

"Not as good as Oren," I declared. Actually, it was not just Oren. Our boys had developed some real teamwork and they were not show-offs. They played hard and they played clean.

"Oren's the best," Jaime chimed in loyally.

"What if we don't win?" Maryjo worried.

I said, "I'll die."

I wouldn't, of course. No one dies over stuff like basketball games unless they have a heart attack or something. But one or more of the high school coaches scouted every game. If he continued to play well, Oren stood a good chance of eventually making it onto the high school team.

Central edged further ahead and held the lead through the third quarter. Then, about midway through the fourth, the score rocketed back and forth between the rivals until I thought I couldn't stand a minute more of suspense. Suddenly we were tied.

Remembering Oren's final-second timing in the other game and forgetting myself, I stood up and screeched, "Oren! Do something!"

Whether or not he even heard was debatable, but the clock had only a few seconds to go and when he got a chance he took it. The ball slipped smoothly over the rim and down and after a short scrimmage in which no one scored, the buzzer blared, announcing the end of the game. Oren had done it again!

Floyd Conner never entered my mind for the rest of that day.

When the phone rang around eight o'clock that evening I was telling Dad for the third time how Oren had practically won the trophy singled-handed. Normally, I got up and answered.

Dad winked at Mom, I kept right on talking, and she got up and went to the phone.

"For you, Pippa," she said a moment later. "Oren Richardson."

"Oren? Mom, are you sure?" Oren had never called me. Boys never did.

Mom's eyes twinkled. "I don't think I'm hard of hearing." I walked a sedate half-dozen steps, rounded the corner out of sight of my parents, snatched up the phone and clapped it against my ear.

"Hello." My voice came out all trembly.

"Hi, P.J. I saw you at the game."

"I saw you for sure. That last basket was awesome."

"Thanks for coming."

"I wouldn't have missed it."

We talked briefly about the game. At least Oren did. I listened and concentrated on restoring my breathing to normal so I wouldn't blow into the phone like Hurricane Hazel.

Oren asked what I'd been up to and I said my biggie was coming up soon and told him about the art contest.

"There's fun stuff going on all over the place," Oren said. "Adoration, the singing group, will be at our church next Saturday night. They're giving a two-hour concert. You want to go with me?"

Would I like to go with him? I'd practically worn out my one Adoration tape, I'd listened to it so much.

Asked a question like that, I couldn't help it. I blew a blast into the phone that could have rivaled any hurricane you could name. "I don't know if my folks will let me," I said. Group activities were still the rule.

"My folks will take us. We'd be at church the whole time, if that makes any difference."

"I'll ask."

I excused myself, asked, and then instead of blowing my breath, I held it.

Mom and Dad looked at each other. "You say you'll be going with his parents?"

"Right."

"And it's at his church?"

"Oren's Baptist. He goes to that brown brick church across from Britton's Nursing Home," I explained.

"Since it's a church function and with his parents, I don't see why not. What do you think, Will?" Mom asked Dad. "Being chaperoned by parents isn't like going off alone with a boy in a car."

The moment Dad agreed, I was off and running. "They said yes—since it's at church and with your parents. Thank you for asking me," I added, remembering my manners.

Oren said, "I just thought of something. My cousin's getting married and Mom has a bridal shower. Dad'll be taking us. I hope that's OK."

"I doubt if the folks will care if it's parent singular or parents plural, just so it's parent."

Oren laughed. "Right."

I said, "Right," and we both laughed and for the rest of the evening my torn-apart world seemed almost normal again.

13

"Pippa, may I ask a favor?" Mom wanted to know on Monday. Evidently she hadn't smelled the cookies I'd baked before she got home.

"What's up?" I asked.

"My second graders are at a vulnerable stage," she explained. "They've learned all kinds of rules for this and that, and they could recite them backwards. I wish I knew how capable they were of translating good rules into action."

"What does that have to do with me?"

She said, "I want you to come and talk to them."

"Oh, sure. That's me—Pippa the profound lecturer. No thanks, Mom."

"I'd help you decide what to say, of course." Mom paused

and her eyes searched mine. "But since your experience with responding to the invitation of a stranger is so recent—"

So that was it! "Forget it, Mom."

Mom stuffed a little bundle of celery into the food processor and touched a button.

"I can get you excused from classes for a couple of hours," she said after it stopped.

"Mom—I said no way!"

"Children often idolize teens, you know—look up to them, long to be like them."

"Mo-om!"

"Just think, Honey, your bad experience might well be turned into good for someone else."

"And my stupidity announced to twenty-four more little kids. No thanks."

"Pippa, it wouldn't be like that. No one thinks you were stupid. We all make mistakes."

I put my hands over my ears, ran to my room, and slammed the door. Why did she have to bring up dumb old Floyd Conner when I was just going to tell her about the art contest?

I laid down on the bed, my mind a jumble of unhappy thoughts. Bit by bit I started to calm down. By the time the aroma of her homemade chicken soup had wafted down the hall, I had decided between two outfits for my date with Oren. At dinner, Mom remembered the art competition.

"Did you finish your entry and hand it in on time?" she asked. I had worked on it most of the weekend.

"Yes, but I saw some of the others. I'm not sure I even stand a chance," I said.

Dad squeezed my hand reassuringly. "You'll do all right," he said. "What I saw of your project bordered on the exceptional."

"You're my dad."

"I also studied art once upon a time," he reminded me.

"Then why aren't you an artist?" Jaime wanted to know.

"Because I'd have to be a very good artist in order to earn a living," he said. "P.J. has more talent in one little finger than I have in ten. You'll place, P.J., even if you don't win."

I wanted to believe him. Still, when I couldn't draw one simple picture for the police—

"Winning isn't everything," I said. "I had *fun* doing this picture, and the teacher likes it."

On Friday I could hardly wait for two o'clock assembly when all our entries would be on display and the winners announced. As students gathered in the gym, you could tell by the noise level that sports and not the fine arts was what was popular. No problem. Probably if I were the only one to enroll, I'd still have chosen to study art.

Since I wasn't expecting to win, or to have a big deal made about it if I did, it came as a huge surprise when the principal got up and made a little speech about "working under the handicap of a broken arm and having to overcome great odds." Then he announced my picture as "best of category." Ten minutes later, I had also walked off with grand prize overall! Most astonishing of all was to see the entire student body stand and clap and whistle as if I'd just shot the winning basket.

Robyn squealed and hugged me and Maryjo shoved me toward the microphone where Mr. Cordell stood clapping along with a group of other winners.

And then it happened. Instead of acting gracious and dignified while I congratulated the others, I started to bawl. Once the tears started, I couldn't stop. Mrs. Shaw, the school counselor, finally came and got me and had me lie down on a couch in the room behind her tiny office.

"It should have been the proudest moment of my entire life and I had to go and blow it," I wailed that evening. "My nose started running and I didn't have a tissue. Now the whole school knows I'm the dork of all dorks."

"How well I remember the year your father got his Master's degree," Mom reminisced. "That too was a proud moment. When the day came, I was so weary from having worked to help him through school, I couldn't even stand up and clap. I just sat in my chair and cried. All I could think about was how relieved I was to have those difficult years behind me."

"Yes, but you were a grownup."

Mom smiled. "With a terribly pink nose for the rest of that wonderful, red-letter day. It's all right to show emotion, Honey."

"Well, it's not OK to act stupid in a public junior high school of all places," I retorted.

"What are you wearing for the concert tomorrow evening?" Mom asked. This from the lady who invariably said that what one wore was not of topmost importance. She had deliberately changed the subject. No problem. To think about proper attire was to think about the concert. And to think about the concert was to think about Oren. To think about Oren was—

I smiled and announced dreamily that I was wavering between the outfit I got for Christmas and the blue dress I knew did things for my pale blue eyes.

The thermometer plunged downward on Saturday so I dropped the notion of enhancing my eyes and opted for the warmer outfit. Since the outfit included a heavy sweater and Oren also wore a sweater, we matched. Sort of, anyhow.

I was ready a full hour ahead of concert time, which turned out to be good timing. Oren came early.

"Dad had to wait for an important phone call," he explained. "He asked if we'd mind taking the bus so we can be sure to get good seats." He looked at Dad. "Is that all right, sir? Dad plans on being there to drive us home."

Obviously impressed with Oren's good manners, Dad said, "Fine, fine, no problem."

As we breathed the crisp, cold air on our way to the bus stop, Oren kept smiling at me and I kept smiling back. I never once thought of Floyd Conner, not even when we reached Fairview and had to wait for our bus.

"It was neat you won yesterday," Oren said a few minutes later as we jostled beside each other on the slow-moving bus.

"Thanks."

Not a word about my tears or humiliation. Apparently my big scene hadn't bothered Oren. I drew a deep breath, smiled again, and kept my mouth shut about it.

The sanctuary of Oren's church was warmly lit and alive with young people from the various churches. Robyn and Maryjo were there along with several other kids from our church. We located seats near center front and saved a place for Oren's dad. When Oren saw him come in and choose a seat elsewhere, we slid over and let someone else have it.

Adoration was all I'd expected and more. A bit loud for the sprinkling of adults in the audience, but who cared? We clapped and sang along when we were asked to, heard testimonies, and listened raptly to the songs of happy praise. After the concert ended, I desired more than ever to honor Jesus Christ by the way that I lived.

"Awesome," Oren turned to me and said following the closing prayer.

The mood changed rapidly, and we were soon busy meeting the members of the singing group and greeting our friends.

"Dad said if we don't make connections inside he'll meet us in the parking lot." Oren told me after the crowd had started to thin. "I don't see him, but I know about where he usually parks."

We'd gone outside and had started toward the parking lot when it struck me. I didn't know Oren's father! My fists made tight little balls inside my coat pockets while I tried to think what to do. I couldn't, not in a million years, just walk out to a dark parking lot and climb into a strange car with a man I'd never seen before in my life.

Oren caught ahold of my arm. "C'mon, slowpoke."

"I—wish your dad had sat with us," I said.

"I thought it was neat of him not to." Oren replied.

I stopped. "I know. I'll go back inside and you go get him. That way we can meet properly before—"

Oren's dark eyebrows formed a single line as he faced me in the semi-darkness. "Before what?"

"Here's Dad now," he said as a cream-colored Buick moved forward on the narrow strip of blacktop and stopped beside us.

A gloved hand reached to open the passenger door. I shrank back into the shadows behind Oren. The roomy car offered plenty of space for three on the front seat.

"You first," Oren said.

"Please, I should—"

I should what? Run? Scream? Call my own dad? The light was on inside the car. A kindly voice said, "Hop in, kids."

Still stalling, I risked a glance at Oren's father and saw a shock of blond hair like Oren's and a wide grin that also matched. This was no stranger. Oren's dad sat on the exact same bleacher at every basketball game and could out-yell everyone else. Nothing about him even resembled Floyd Conner.

"Hello," I said somewhat tremulously, sliding across the seat, making room for Oren. "I'm Pippa Howard, P.J. for short."

"Nice to meet you, P.J.," Oren's father said. "They call me

Rich, but you may call me Mr. Richardson, parent singular, if you'd like."

He was teasing, of course. I giggled. Then I almost choked. The giggle was genuine enough, but so filled with relief it sounded like a clogged drinking fountain.

What's more, Oren must really have like me a lot to have repeated something I'd said to his father of all people.

14

At home, Oren walked with me to the door, squeezed both of my hands, and said, "I liked being with you." He leaped off the step and rejoined his father in the car.

I floated into the house, said good night to my parents, slept like a baby, and talked about Oren all through breakfast and Sunday dinner. By Sunday afternoon I was back down in the dumps.

Anyone who could carry off the top awards in an art competition, I reasoned as I got out paper and pencil, ought also to be able to draw a simple picture.

To get myself in the mood, I drew a caricature of George Bush and one of Oren shooting baskets. George got shoved aside. I tacked Oren in the center of my bulletin board. As I sat on the edge of the bed thinking about what it had been like going out with him, it started to itch under my cast.

I slid a letter opener under it and scratched the parts I could reach. My elbow had driven me crazy for about a week. Two more weeks, Dr. Thorpe said, and he'd take it off. I could hardly wait.

I doodled across the top of my art pad with a sharp pencil. Sighing, I set to work and quickly drew the thick gray hair. Next I did the outline of a face and sketched in a nose I thought might be about right. Without stopping, I added eyes and a mouth. I held the pad at arm's length, looked at it, and ripped the page off and stuffed it into my wastebasket. Rapid drawing had failed again.

I sauntered out to the family room where Mom sat working on a crossword puzzle. Dad was asleep on the couch with the Sunday-school paper over his face. Jaime was outside on the deck, jumping rope.

"I give up. I'll never in a trillion years be able to draw that dumb picture. As of today, right this minute, I quit," I announced to all who might be listening.

"I'm sorry," Mom began.

"Besides, I can be in a really good mood, I mean a *really* good mood and then—I am not going to waste another Sunday afternoon on creepy old Floyd Conner and that's final."

Dad slid the Sunday-school paper aside. "Why'd you pick a depressing project like Conner for a Sunday afternoon? Sunday's a day for rest and worship and gladness, not for gloom and doom," he reminded.

"I've been busy!" I snapped.

Dad looked sober.

"OK. So I keep putting it off. Wouldn't you?" I challenged.

"I would for a fact," he said. "So why don't you? I suggest you ignore it, forget it, let it slide clean out of your brain."

I giggled. "Oh, Daddy."

He sat up and smoothed his hair with his long fingers. "It's spring. Look at the sunshine. Grab your sweatsuit and go with me for a run to the park and back."

With my cast and my short legs, running with Dad was like an elderly dachshund trying to keep pace with a trained greyhound, but I had nothing better to do. I said OK and went in and changed my clothes.

"Wear your old tennies, both of you," Mom called. "It's muddy."

The park was about six blocks from our house so, although I mostly walked or jogged, I was puffing long before we arrived.

"How about twice around the fountain and then home?" Dad suggested, breaking pace.

"Only if we stop and rest," I gasped, remembering a picnic table on the opposite side of the fountain.

"Once around and you'll have earned your stop," he promised.

The picnic table with its attached benches turned out to be already occupied.

As Dad slowed and called out, "Hi, neighbors," I recognized Davida's parents, who were also dressed for running. "Mind if we light for a minute?" Dad asked.

"Hello, Mr. Rochelle, Mrs. Rochelle," I said, plopping onto the bench opposite them and leaning my heaving chest against the cold cement table.

"Winter, plus not enough exercise, leaves one out of shape," Mr. Rochelle remarked.

The Rochelles were anything but out of shape. They were as slim and attractive as any of the parents I knew. Dressed in matching gray sweatsuits, they also wore gray running shoes. As always, Mrs. Rochelle's hair and fingernails looked like the ads in Mom's *Good Housekeeping* magazine.

They spoke with Dad a bit about the weather before Mrs. Rochelle turned to me and asked. "How are you doing these days, Pippa Jean? Has your world managed to right itself again?"

"I'm OK," I said.

I could tell by the way she looked at me she knew better.

"Any leads yet on that scoundrel?" Mr. Rochelle asked.

Dad said, "Not really. It's been so long now I'm beginning to wonder if the investigators will ever catch up with him. Man's slippery as the proverbial eel."

"It's a concern, isn't it?" Mrs. Rochelle remarked. "I'm sure no one will ever fool our Pippa again. Nevertheless, I worry about the other children of this city."

The familiar ugliness had started to spread like poison inside me. A tiny moan escaped my lips. "If I hadn't been so stupid, it never would have happened," I said. "It's my fault."

Mrs. Rochelle's eyes darkened with concern. "No, Pippa," she said quite firmly. "It's not your fault."

"Yes it is."

"No, Pippa."

"It's what everyone thinks, what some have even said," I insisted.

"Who?" she probed. "Surely no one in their right mind." Since Mrs. Rochelle was her mother, I could hardly tell her Davida had been the main one to imply that the encounter with Floyd Conner had been all my fault.

"Lots of people," I lied, not looking at her.

"Are you sure they said it, or is it what you think they might be saying behind your back?" Mrs. Rochelle asked gently.

Davida had said it. I picked a splinter off the wooden bench and broke it into bits. "Most—I guess it's what I think they might be saying," I admitted.

Mrs. Rochelle asked me a long list of questions and Mr. Rochelle interrupted once in a while to ask one of his own. As I had done with everyone else, I answered truthfully.

Once, when the probing got a bit heavy, Mr. Rochelle

smiled at Dad and said. "Don't worry. No charge, not for good neighbors."

Then it dawned on me that here were two neighbors who were also good doctors. Right there on that park bench I was being treated as professionally as if I'd been laying on a couch in their office—or whatever it is they do with patients when they're dealing with problems.

Finally, Mr. Rochelle reached across the table and lifted my chin with a perfectly manicured finger. "Pippa, you must believe what I am about to say. You must believe it with all your heart and mind."

"I'll try," I promised.

"Floyd Conner is the person with the problem. You are the victim. If he had not found you, lied to you, he would soon have found some other unsuspecting person. You simply happened to be there. It could have happened to anyone, Pippa—to Davida, or even to her mom or yours. Men with problems like his are seldom selective. It's whoever happens along at the convenient moment. You must believe that, Pippa."

"If that's so, and I'm not saying it isn't," I said, wanting very much to believe him, "then how come I didn't try to get away sooner? Why did I have to wait till we got clear out to Riverside Park?"

"Fear causes a variety of behavioral reactions, Pippa. Knowing you and your family, and because I am aware of your strong religious beliefs, I suspect that right up to the last you wanted very much to believe the best about Conner. You hoped you were wrong as to what he might do. You were willing to give him every chance in your book to turn around and drive you back to that office. It's as simple as that."

What Mr. Rochelle said made sense. The awful squiggliness had subsided.

"I guess now that you've heard it from the doctors, you

can cease with calling yourself names every time the subject comes up," Dad commented dryly.

"OK. I am not stupid. I am not stupid. I am not stupid. Is that better?" I asked, feeling more lighthearted than I had in weeks.

"Much. Thanks, neighbors—friends," Dad said, reaching out with both hands and grasping the outstretched hands of both of the Rochelles.

I hopped up. "Race you home," I said and was off before Dad could untangle his legs.

He caught up with me on the second lap around the fountain and I was puffing worse than ever by the time we got home. But I felt good, exuberant, in fact.

"It's been ages since I've had any friends over," I said after I'd had a drink and cooled off some. "Spring break is week after next. That's when I get my cast off. Could I celebrate with a sleepover?"

Mom hugged me. "P.J., that's a great idea."

Then, while Dad hugged her, I ran to the phone and called Maryjo and then Robyn.

15

"I used to think adults were like furniture, not someone you could talk to," I said to Maryjo as we strolled home from school the next Monday.

The day was gorgeous, springlike, and so warm we had our sweaters tied around our waists. Maryjo had to tie mine because I still had my cast.

"I don't mean Mom and Dad," I added. "I've always talked to them."

"You haven't always wanted to," Maryjo reminded.

"True. But you'll have to admit, even if you've always trusted someone all your life, some subjects are harder to discuss."

"Right."

"I have you to thank for helping me to realize how important it was to confide in my folks. I'd never have made it through all this without them—or you. It's Davida's parents I'm talking about, however." I told Maryjo about meeting them in the park.

"I honestly believed Davida when she suggested all that happened with Floyd Conner was my fault," I said. "Interesting that they should be the ones to help me get my head on straight."

"Davida's a spoiled brat," Maryjo said. "She's an only child, don't forget. And her folks don't go to church or anything. Their values are different." I didn't enjoy talking about people. Besides, after Sunday, I had started to feel differently about Davida's family.

We lingered at the end of our driveway. Maryjo asked about Oren. As always, hearing his name was almost as good as saying it. I seldom talked about Oren with my folks because Dad liked to tease and Mom gave little lectures about getting too serious.

"He's coming over after dinner to help me with grammar."

Maryjo's hands flew to her hips. "Pippa Jean Howard, you get the best grades in class!"

"What's that have to do with anything?" I asked nonchalantly. "Do you think he'd like brownies or should I bake chocolate chip?"

"How would I know, you lucky duck."

Sometimes I forgot about Maryjo's liking Oren too.

"I might as well have invited you in," I said after we'd yakked a while longer. "It must be about time for Jaime's bus."

"Past," Maryjo said, after looking at her watch. Jaime's bus was never late. Without looking, I could tell time practically to the minute when Jaime would bounce down the steps, run to the house, fling her papers on the table, and grab her jump rope.

"I wonder what's wrong?"

"Silly. A late bus doesn't have to mean something's wrong."

"What time is it?"

"Exactly seven minutes and ten—no, five—seconds to four."

"Jaime's always home by 3:45."

"Pippa the worrywart. Jaime's fine. Relax."

I did my best. After Maryjo left, I went inside the empty house and got out stuff for making brownies. When I remembered Oren sometimes had a problem with zits, I got out peanut butter instead.

At 4:10, Jaime still hadn't come home.

At 4:11, I called her school office and was informed that all the buses had left on time. "Don't worry. Traffic's often to blame," an impersonal voice on the other phone said.

I hung up and measured brown sugar. Should I call Mom? Dad? Or both?

A bird lit on the topmost branch of the rose bush beneath the kitchen window and pecked at a lingering seed pod. *I caught me a little brown bird once—*

The eerie, singsong voice of Floyd Conner pounded inside my head. What if while Maryjo and I dawdled, the bus had arrived? I had my own house key. Jaime did not. Supposing Floyd Conner had happened along and found her waiting outside the house alone?

I picked up the beaters and then laid them back on the counter. Fingers trembling, I dialed Garfield's number.

"Jaime's not home," I blurted after they'd finally located Mom in the parking lot where she'd been about to start home. Then I began to cry—deep, gulping sobs.

"P.J.!" She was practically shouting. "Hush!"

I hushed, at least enough to hear.

"Today was Jaime's field trip."

I had forgotten. They were going to the zoo.

"They were going to get to stay and help feed the animals. She won't be home until after five."

Feeling a trifle embarrassed, I apologized. "I was sure old what's-his-face had kidnapped her right off the bus," I said in a feeble attempt at lightness.

It grew quiet on her end of the line. Then, "Honey, aren't you ever even going to try to put all that out of your mind? I don't suppose that man even knows you have a little sister."

She was right, of course—at least I hoped she was. Still, I went right on thinking dark thoughts about him all the time I was mixing the cookies.

At 5:05, Jaime bounced in and chattered incessantly about feeding apples to elephants. Mom arrived ten minutes later. Once again, my world had turned right side up.

But Mom had been right. I must do something about the way I kept getting scared over nothing. If I didn't, I'd go crazy. After Oren left that night, I called Gwen.

"Blizzards are on special this week at the DQ," she said. "How about tomorrow night at seven? My treat."

"No, mine." I had worked quite a few hours. Besides, Gwen had given me more than a fair share of time. "It's my turn to do something nice for you," I said, and added, "There's the small matter of no DL of course. You'll have to pick me up." Actually, I didn't expect to get a driver's license until I was at least sixteen, but it was the in thing to speak of it as if getting a license were just around the corner.

At the Dairy Queen, I ordered a large Blizzard and then wondered how I could possibly eat that much chocolate chunk ice cream at one sitting (I managed).

I liked Gwen. She never whipped out her college psych or soc or anything else and tried it on you. She came straight at you with practical, down-to-earth ideas or advice, often through a Scripture verse. Sometimes she'd simply tell an anecdote or Bible story and allow it to sink in.

She took a bite of her Blizzard, savoring it. "Pippa, how

many times do you suppose you've heard the story of Joseph?"

I shrugged. "Who knows?"

"Just for fun, let's count. How many at home?"

"Hundreds." Besides family devotions and bedtime stories, I had a tape. Jaime still listened to it.

"Give it two hundred," Gwen said. "And at Sunday school?"

"We made coats of many colors every time we turned around. Give me a box of felt tips and I could make a striped coat in my sleep," I said.

"And the rest of the story? Probably not quite so often?"

"Often enough so I could tell it to you backwards."

"Let's hear you."

"Not now. I'm eating. I never tell anything backwards while I'm eating."

We both knew when the moment came to cease with silliness.

"But I'm not like Joseph," I said. "He was always good. He always did the right thing at the right time."

Gwen started shaking her head before I'd hardly begun.

"Joseph, I think, was his daddy's darling—maybe even a bit of a spoiled brat. Or, at the very least, a know-it-all. He was like a flea in the ear to his big brothers, a pesty kid with a braggy mouth."

I thought Gwen was being a bit hard on a genuine Bible hero, but I kept my opinion to myself.

She went on. "The part worth noticing is that Joseph didn't remain a brat. At some point he knuckled down and started to grow up. Maybe the same day his brothers chucked him into that pit."

Melting Blizzard dripped from my spoon. "Are you saying I'm a spoiled brat who needs to grow up?"

Gwen's eyes held mine. "No. P.J. You are neither spoiled nor a brat. You are quite responsible. You are one of the few I can always count on to act your age and even to be Christlike when faced with a crisis. We're talking about Joseph because of all the trouble he went through."

"You mean pit, van, what's the dif?"

"Not quite. Actually, I suspect Joseph hunkered down in the bottom of that pit and whimpered and bawled as loudly as you or I ever could or would. I think too he must have been scared spitless when Potiphar's wife snatched onto him like she did. No, what I'm thinking about is the good that eventually came about because Joseph allowed God to work in his life.

"Joseph was his daddy's favorite. Do you think Pop would ever have agreed to his moving away? I doubt it. But because Joseph ended up exactly where he was needed, God was able to put his talents and abilities to work for the benefit of others. Could that have happened, do you think, without that pit experience?"

"No. And I see what you're saying."

Still, I wasn't sure I believed that God had actually allowed Floyd Conner into my life to do what he did. I said so.

"I'm not blaming God for anything. Who knows or understands His ways? Not I," Gwen said. "All I'm saying is, OK, P.J., this terrible thing happened to you, seemingly for no worthwhile reason.

"The fact is, it *did* happen. Now as I see it, you can let that defeat you and keep you scared for the rest of your life. Or you can say, 'OK, God, the worst is over, the best is yet to come. How would You like to turn my bad experience into good for me or for someone else?'"

Gwen had given me something new to think about. She drove me home and took time to pray for me in the car before I got out. I thoughtfully went inside and dressed for bed.

16

Maryjo and Robyn slept over on Sunday night at the start of spring break. We stayed awake until after 1:00 P.M. and slept until noon the next day. Mom made us waffles from scratch (she hardly ever did) and I got to microwave a whole package of bacon just for the three of us.

On Thursday, I got my cast off.

"Phew!" I said, grabbing my nose and holding it.

"Smells a bit, doesn't it?" Dr. Thorpe remarked.

"Not only that, it stinks," I said.

"Well, you can wash it as often as you like now. It looks good, really good," he said, turning and bending my arm, examining it carefully.

"The skin's weird," I said.

"That will change," he assured me.

My arm would be skinny and white and shrively for Maryjo's party that night, but it couldn't be helped. I would also have to carry along my little bottle of lotion for whenever it itched.

What my friends and I called parties were not really parties at all, but times when we invited a group instead of one or two and planned a definite time and place to get together. Maryjo's guest list seldom varied. Like mine, if I was the one giving the party, it generally consisted of church kids.

We didn't do it that way to exclude anyone, but because of all we had in common. Kids who drank or did drugs ran around together, as did those who were into computers. Our common bond had to do with knowing Jesus Christ and wanting to please Him even when we were goofing around.

To help me celebrate the liberation of my arm and elbow, Maryjo invited Oren. So he wouldn't feel funny being the only one not from our youth group, she included another boy and girl from his church. While I preferred to think it wouldn't have mattered as long as I was there, it was thoughtful of Maryjo to invite them.

We sat on the floor and played Pictionary. I was still the artist, but it was Oren who kept us laughing with his crazy, jabby drawings.

When I asked Maryjo later on in the kitchen if she thought I'd embarrassed him by laughing too loudly, she said, "How could you help it? He's so neat. Like I said—"

I gave her a quick hug. "Yes, I know. If I didn't already like him, you would be first in line."

"Right."

While I ran the air popper, Maryjo dumped cookies into a bowl and set out pop. We watched a couple of old Laurel and Hardy flicks and then our parents started arriving. Since it was only a block and a half to where I lived, I walked. I'd hoped Oren would offer to walk with me, but his mom was among the first to arrive and the other kids from his church rode home with them.

At home, I stretched out on my bed, enjoying the luxury of raising my left arm above my head. "Thank you, Jesus, for a special night," I said out loud. I hugged myself with both arms and smiled.

I had first gotten to know Oren during a classroom session when we had both been assigned to the same group. We ate lunch together sometimes and he often walked me to class. I had not missed a single home game and I knew how much he liked basketball. Sitting next to him at the concert, I had sensed his allegiance to Jesus Christ. Tonight I had watched how he played.

As I turned off my light, I wished I would never have to think about anyone or anything besides Oren and growing up to be a really good artist.

Jesus would still be first, of course, and I'd include my family and friends and other activities I enjoyed, but the bad stuff would all go away.

The week of vacation ended. When we got back to school, all we eighth graders could talk about was how soon we'd be in ninth. At home, Dad's biggest day of the year (April 15) came and went. While he still had much to do. he said it was time to knock off early for one evening and celebrate.

Friday night he made reservations at La Fiesta and took us all out for Mexican buffet. I stuffed myself on chicken enchilada and we all put on huge brimmed hats and had our picture taken. A man with very white teeth and a mandolin stopped at our table and sang a Mexican song of celebration.

After dinner, Dad had to join his bowling team as usual so we dropped him off and went on to the mall. This time, instead of asking for more barrettes, Jaime begged to buy a cowboy hat she saw in a window display. When Mom said no, Jaime asked, "What are we going to buy?"

108

Mom said, "I thought we'd look at summer clothes."

Summer? Already? Still, in a way, years had passed in the last three months.

At 8:45, when a few of the less-busy shops had drawn steel grids across their fronts, we left and went to the bowling alley.

"You're early," Dad said, greeting us and locating a place for us to sit. "But that's just great. I'm not doing so well. I can use a cheering section."

"Too many burritos," Mom remarked.

She was teasing, of course. Dad never overate. Mom did and I did, but Dad said more people died with a fork in the mouth than with a knife in the back. Personally, when that time came around, I'd choose the fork—loaded perhaps with a cheesy bit of chicken enchilada laced with hot sauce.

Moments later, I wished myself already dead or at least as far away as South Africa.

The empty seats Dad found for us happened to be right behind where he sat with his team. I had just taken off my coat when the man who'd been bowling finished his turn. As he walked back to his seat, I recognized him as the person I'd mistaken once before for Floyd Conner.

Startled at what I knew to be more than a passing likeness, I must have been staring when suddenly his eyes caught mine. For a split second he stared back.

As he dropped into a vinyl-clad seat and began talking and laughing with the men closest to him, I could almost hear the wild beating of my heart.

Except, how could he possibly be Floyd Conner? Dressed in neat slacks and a sharp-looking red bowling shirt with Tyson Manufacturing written across the back in white letters, this man was as bald as I'd remembered him from before.

His back was practically to me now. I swallowed and gripped the chair arms.

Arms folded across the back of the seat in front of her,

Jaime sat on the edge of her chair. Suddenly she pointed. She said, "Look at those funny boots, P.J."

I leaned forward to look and immediately froze. Beneath the man's chair was a pair of cowboy boots. Weird boots. Terrible boots. Boots with brass tips and red and green stones and the twisting forms of a serpent and a mermaid.

Too terrified to move or to speak, I sat for a moment, my thoughts whirling like dust devils.

What time I am afraid, I will trust.

The Bible verse I had learned when I was younger than Jaime seemed to come from nowhere. It hadn't, of course. While I had not had time to think it through, God was there and I knew instinctively that He would see me through whatever was ahead.

An expired coupon for a free Pepsi lay on the seat beside me. I picked it up. Forcing my trembling fingers to work slowly, I fashioned it into a tiny yellow airplane.

"May I have it?" Jaime asked, leaning across Mom's lap to watch.

"Not yet. I need to add some windows and a name," I said. Probably no one was watching or could have heard above all the noise, but I had to make sure. Jaime settled back to wait.

"Mom," I scribbled as fast as I could. "I *know* the bald man sitting beside Ralph H. is Floyd Conner. Should we call the police?"

Dad was bowling now and Jaime was watching him. I touched Mom's hand and pointed discreetly to what I had written.

She read it and gasped. "How—" she started to mouth.

"Ssssh!" I hissed back.

A small eternity passed while we watched and waited for Dad to complete his turn. I erased the note and drew a circle with a star, printed some numbers, named the airplane

Yellow Jacket, and handed it to Jaime. When Dad made a strike, we all clapped.

"I'll go get us something to drink," Mom said, standing, moving calmly away as if nothing were wrong.

Normally, Jaime would have jumped up and tagged along. The airplane had captured her attention and was keeping her occupied.

"You forgot to put a star on both sides," she said as Mom was leaving.

I too wanted to run after Mom, to keep right on going, to get as far away from Floyd Conner as possible.

Forcing my hands to be still, I drew a second star. Then I fixed my eyes on the huge round clock advertising Dr. Pepper. The second hand crept slowly around. Once. Twice. Three times. Four—

Cold air hit the back of my neck. The outside door closed. Jaime turned around.

"Hey, Mom's talk—"

I clapped a hand over her mouth, said, "Your barrette's falling out," and hissed in her ear, "Keep still!"

Her eyes were like silver dollars. Miraculously, she did as she was told. What's more, I'd spoken the truth about the barrette. But then she always has one hanging someplace. I reached to fasten it.

Two police officers sauntered across the back of the seating area and started down the short aisle to where the bald-headed man was seated. He looked up and saw them, started to get up, then sat back down.

A ball crashed in the next alley, making a strike. I couldn't hear a word, but as one officer spoke, I saw Floyd Conner glance furtively at me.

He knew who I was! He knew I was watching! Suddenly, as if reaching for his wallet, he leaned forward, dropped to all fours and scrambled between the officers. Rising quickly, he took a step toward the aisle, his only way of escape.

They were on him in an instant.

Dad. I wanted to be near Dad, to feel his protection. As I started to get up and go to him, my knees buckled. The room swirled and righted itself.

The ordeal was a long way from being over, but the worst had ended for me. Floyd Conner had at last been apprehended.

17

During the days following his arrest, Floyd Conner confessed both to my abduction and to having abducted other young girls in other places.

His name was not Floyd at all—or Max Dunfelt or any of three other aliases—but Joe Harding. Fear of detection had kept him on the move and he had lived in our area for less than a year. He'd taken mostly factory jobs where few questions were asked and which were easy to walk away from.

For days, Floyd's was the top story on the front page of *The Chronicle* and on TV news. Turn on the radio and you got Floyd along with the disc jockeys.

"I didn't mean no harm," he blubbered to the investigative reporter from Channel 6. "But I get these crazy spells."

Except for what he repeatedly referred to as "crazy spells," Floyd led a quiet and probably lonely life in a small rented house just south of the city. He drove a modest Ford Escort back and forth to his assembly line job at Tyson Manufacturing. Bowling appeared to be his only outside interest and one of the men at the factory had had to talk him into that.

A search of the house and outbuildings turned up a variety of wigs, including the gray one. Under the bed were boxes stuffed with assorted articles of clothing Floyd used to complete his disguise. Scattered throughout the house, and stuffed in drawers and closets, police found hundreds of copies of pornographic magazines.

Pictures of the dilapidated building where he stored the old white van appeared on the front page of the paper. Sagging doors and a lush growth of summer's now-dried weeds made it easy for him to keep the van hidden.

"I still can't figure out why I couldn't draw that picture," I said to Chief Gage the day he stopped by just to see how I was doing. "The minute I recognized that creepy cowboy boot, every detail of his face came back in a flash."

"I've seen fear leave folks speechless," Chief Gage said. "At least you could still talk—and you helped a lot. You especially helped us by keeping a clear head there at the bowling alley when you recognized him."

"I still wish I could have done as you asked."

Chief Gage smiled reassuringly. "Well, it's overwith now. And there could come a time when all you've been through will turn out to be helpful to someone else. You never know."

Supposedly, the matter was over and done with. But with the media offering a daily dose of Floyd Conner, how was I ever going to forget and get on with my life?

One thing we learned was that Floyd had a lot of problems. During their high school years both he and a friend had been unsuccessful at dating, and the friend had insisted that it was no sweat—that there were other ways to "enjoy" girls.

That friend who first introduced Floyd to pornography had soon outgrown the stuff, graduated from high school, then college, and was now raising a family. Floyd, however, had been hooked for life. Eventually, he had started acting out some of what was suggested by the magazines. Outwardly, he led a respectable life. He was a good neighbor and an excellent workman. Those who worked beside him at Tyson could hardly believe that the Joe Harding they knew was so twisted inside.

As the investigation continued, and more and more was revealed, Dad said, "I still can't believe I bowled almost every week alongside Tyson's team and never once suspected. The Joe Harding I've known since October was a nice man."

"What I'm wondering," Mom asked, "is, why our P.J.? What caused him to choose her? And how was it he knew so much about her—about us?"

Dad said, "I think what they're finding out is that what Floyd—Joe—calls his 'crazy spells' are really carefully thought out plans. He's smart, but he has a sick, sick mind. We in our right minds can't begin to understand the thinking of a person like Conner."

"You can say that again!" I muttered.

Dad continued. "He was a stranger in town and a loner. I doubt if he was acquainted with any young people. But he's no dummy. With all the blitz about talking to strangers, he knew he couldn't con just any girl into getting into a car with him. He had to know something about her, find some reason for her to trust him. You'll have to hand it to him—the guy did his homework." Dad sighed. "Maybe if I'd resisted the urge to brag to the guys at Tipenny's, he'd never have known about Pippa's helping out at the office."

"Dad, all great fathers brag about their wonderful kids," I interjected with a smile.

"True. But I still never dreamed anyone would pick up on that detail."

Mom said, "Who knows? Maybe he noted the color or cut of P.J.'s coat—or that horrible old plaid scarf."

"Mom, I *like* that scarf," I protested. Then, "You know, I'll always hate what happened, but I feel kind of sorry for the man, don't you?"

Dad's expression was noncommittal. "Don't go feeling too sorry for him, Honey. He's where he deserves to be. He also needs to be kept where he can no longer hurt anyone."

I blinked back tears. "Oh, I know that, Dad. He belongs in jail. And I'm glad he's in jail. I also know I need to forgive him. Probably I'm in the middle of doing that. If he was to get out, I know I'd still be afraid of him, but he still needs help."

Pastor Henley goes to see him almost every day," Dad said, and added. "We must pray for him. He's been our pastor since before you were born. Visiting Conner can't be easy for him."

Unnoticed, Jaime had come in and was sitting quietly on the edge of the couch. "Why not?" she said. "It's a Jesus kind of a thing to do."

"Out of the mouths of babes," Dad said, tousling her hair until the barrettes started to drop.

That began another discussion. Not the barrettes, but the fact that he'd implied Jaime might still be a baby.

Remembering how often she had comforted me while I was hurting, I said, "Jaime's growing up, Dad. She's no longer my baby sister. We're just—sisters."

I too had done a heap of growing up, and Mom had tiny lines around her mouth that I had never noticed before.

Later on, still thinking some about Mom, I moseyed into the bedroom where she was sorting out winter clothes for dry cleaning.

"OK if I lay on the bed?" I asked.

116

"This once," she replied, her mind occupied with the pile of sweaters on the floor.

I laid down on my back and stared at the ceiling. Before saying a word, I had to be quite sure about what I'd been thinking.

"Something on your mind, P.J.?" she asked after the sweaters had been sorted.

"Sort of."

"I'm listening."

After a little while when I still hadn't said anything more, Mom stopped what she was doing and sat down on the edge of the bed. I rolled over and swung my legs around to sit beside her.

"Remember the story of Joseph?" I asked.

"Mmm."

"Gwen and I talked about it the other day."

"It's a wonderful story."

"I've been thinking—actually, it was Gwen who got me started—about the part where Joseph says to his brothers how when they left him in that pit to die, they had in mind to get even with him by getting rid of him. But that turned out to be God's way of moving Joseph to where God needed him to be later on."

"Right."

"Gwen said Joseph was Jacob's favorite. Jacob probably never would have allowed Joseph to go."

"Probably not. We parents can be like that."

"After Gwen and I talked about it, I came home and read the whole story all over again. I couldn't believe how many thousands of people were fed—and lives saved—because Joseph was in Egypt at the right time.

"It's always good to be where God wants us to be," Mom said.

"Chief Gage said something the other day that goes along the same line. He said maybe sometime I could be a help to someone else. Mom—if you still want me to, I think I'd like to talk to your class."

Mom glanced questioningly at me. "Are you sure? You don't have to, you know."

"I'm sure. Just give me some time to think about what to say."

"Perhaps you can jot your thoughts down and I'll take a look and tell you whether or not it's appropriate for second graders. How's that?"

I was about to go to sleep that night when I was struck by a terrific idea. I switched on my bedside lamp, got up, and padded across the soft carpet to my desk. I quietly opened the second drawer, took out art supplies, and began to draw.

It was past midnight when I crawled back into bed, pulled the covers up to my chin, and dropped quickly off to sleep.

The next morning when I showed my sketches to Mom, she said, "That's perfect! What a special way to get a message across!"

"I thought I might use a big flip chart and make each drawing large enough so it can be seen all over the classroom," I told her.

"Good idea."

"With pictures, I wouldn't have to say very much. I'd do captions and maybe some dialog balloons, but I'm not too good with writing."

Mom's eyes sparkled with excitement. "If I promise to help with the writing, or find someone who can, how soon can you have all this ready?"

I shrugged. "I dunno. Cartoons with only a few details are quick and easy. Maybe next week."

I couldn't believe how easy it all seemed. But then, Floyd Conner was in jail and I was safe and a whole lot of people had helped me.

18

"Hey, I saw you on TV," a small boy minus one front tooth remarked the afternoon I walked into Mom's classroom.

"That's right, Derek," Mom said.

She introduced me to her class. "If you listened to the news story, you probably remember that the story about Pippa was not a happy one. Today she's going to tell you what happened. She also plans to show you some ways to protect yourself should anything like that ever happen to you."

I got a little nervous when the principal came in and sat down to listen. Then, in my eagerness to get my message across to the children, I forgot she was even there.

A grubby hand shot in the air. "Yeah, but how you gonna know if the stranger is a bad guy or a good guy?"

"Keep watching," I said, turning the page and reading Mom's carefully worded caption. "The answer is, you won't always know. That's why it's important never to get in a car or accept a treat or even to stand around talking to someone you don't know.

"One problem with a bad stranger is they will lie to you. That's what happened to me. Since I had never seen this person before—at least not that I could remember—it was wrong to stay and talk to him. That gave him time to think up a really big lie.

"You see, I thought I had never seen him before because he was wearing a disguise—a gray wig that made him look like an old man. But he had seen me. My dad sometimes went bowling the same time he did. Sometimes Mom and my sister and I went to watch Dad bowl. The man had talked with Dad. He had seen me there and heard Dad say my name. Do you think you might believe someone who knew your dad and even knew your nickname?"

The presentation took longer than its allotted half hour because of all the questions. Some of the children were curious about my arm, which was still skinnier than the other one. Most had a certain picture they wanted to ask about.

"I've never seen my second graders quite so solemn about a subject," Mom said as we drove home.

"You know, I got a bigger kick out of using my drawings today than I did when I won the contest," I told her.

"Being useful, helping others, brings a kind of satisfaction one cannot experience in any other way," Mom replied.

"Of course I can't take all the credit. You really helped me a lot and I really had to pray before I could get up enough courage."

"Keep those charts," Mom said as I carried them into the house a little while later. "Other teachers may want to invite you for their classrooms."

The next day I was doing homework when Mom called me from her school. She sounded excited.

"As soon as Jaime gets home, the two of you catch a bus and come over to Garfield. Mrs. Cramer would like to see you. Jaime can stay in my classroom and help me finish up for the day while you're talking to her." Mrs. Cramer was her principal.

"Didn't she like what I did yesterday?"

"Quite the opposite," Mom said. "But I'll let her tell you."

Mrs. Cramer's office was as neat and polished-looking as she was. She shook my hand and offered me a chair facing her desk, as if I were totally grown up.

"You did a superb job yesterday, Pippa Jean," she began.

"Thank you," I replied, feeling a bit shy.

"Your illustrations were so good, in fact, I asked your mother if I might speak to you about them."

"I'm glad you liked them."

"I have a friend who works for Artifax—a buyer."

I recognized the name of a small publishing place located in the downtown area.

She went on. "Artifax publishes more than just greeting cards and notepapers. Occasionally they do books, more often they do booklets.

"I talked to my friend about your illustrations, Pippa. He and I both think a booklet could be useful—for homes and libraries as well as schools. He wants to see your drawings."

It got so quiet in her office she could probably hear me breathing. At last I managed to blurt, "He does?"

"I took the liberty of making an appointment for next Thursday after school—of course with the understanding that if you're not interested we will cancel it."

"Oh, no, don't do that!" I said before I could stop myself.

"You like the idea?"

I nodded. "Mom did the captions," I said. "She and her friend."

"Yes, and she'll be given proper credit. But she and I agree—the illustrations are what make the thing sparkle.

"If it's all right with your parents, I'll pick you up at 3:15 next Thursday. My friend's name is Gary Dunstan. Bring your flip chart and we'll see what he has to say about it."

She smiled and I knew I was dismissed.

Mom acted as excited as I was. "Just think, you might get to be a published illustrator long before you've even finished art school!" she said after I'd more or less floated back to her room.

On the way home I came back down to earth when Mom asked, "Isn't this the night Davida's supposed to stay over?"

I groaned. Why Davida on the most triumphant day of my whole life? But her folks had a seminar and they had done a lot for me and it wasn't as though they'd asked at the last minute. With all that had happened, I had simply forgotten.

Whenever I had something neat to tell, I almost always waited and told my best friends first. But the very thought of maybe being published was so exciting I couldn't wait. I told Davida.

Instead of putting me down, she surprised me by asking what the title would be and what name would I use.

I hadn't had time to think about those things.

"Well, think about it," she said, and hugged me as if she truly was glad all this was happening to me.

Perhaps Davida was no different from anyone else after all. Or maybe, like me, she had started to grow up and think about other people instead of herself all the time.

We talked about titles. "Probably Mrs. Cramer's friend will help me with that," I said. "If he decides to publish it."

We turned our attention to how I would sign it. Pippa Jean Howard? P.J. Howard?

"You know if you do become an illustrator, you might want to come up with a really neat name—something eyecatching—like Flavia, who does those cards," Davida suggested.

We thought for a moment and then she grabbed me. "I know! How about Pippa J. Pics? Or P.J. Pics. Maybe Pics by Pippa?"

We tried the names out on Mom and Dad. They both said they liked Pippa J. Pics best. "We named you Pippa because it's such a special, different kind of name," Mom said. "This may be why."

The next day I stayed after school and told my art teacher all about my appointment with Gary Dunstan. Maryjo had the flu so I had to walk home alone anyhow.

Miss Pierce was delighted. "And proud to be your teacher however it turns out," she said, and asked, "How's your arm?"

"Today it hurts," I said. "It always does when it's cold or if it rains." Rain had fallen steadily all day.

Leaving the school a little while later, I hunched inside my thin cotton jacket and wished I'd thought to bring an umbrella. I had gone less than a block before my arms and shoulders were soaked. There was nothing to do but hurry.

I was steaming along, practically running when I heard a car squeal around the corner behind me. It careened past, stopped with a jerk and backed up and stopped beside me.

The front door swung open and a lanky boy holding a beer can hollered, "Wanna ride?"

I peered through the steamy windows. At least two of the boys were in my classes, though I didn't really know any of them. They belonged to a different crowd.

I had started to shiver. If I hadn't already done so, I was probably going to catch cold. Maybe I'd have to miss my appointment with the editor. My arm felt as if it had been run over all over again. I took a step toward the car.

"C'mon, get in where it's warm," a boy in the back seat coaxed.

They all laughed and the boy with the beer tipped his can up and took a drink.

"Aren't you cold, Sweetheart?"

Something clicked inside my head. *Never again, stupid.* Ashamed to have hesitated, I lifted my chin, smiled briefly at the boys and said, "I'm fine. I like rain. Thanks, but no thanks."

As I turned and walked on toward home, maybe I imagined it, but the cold rain seemed suddenly warmer. Or perhaps it was because I'd just gotten another idea.

Would *Thanks, But No Thanks* be a good title for our book about strangers?